B

W

MW01141090

FOUND: LOVE

A

Tennessee: Love

Romance

Other books by Donna Wright:

The *Tennessee: Love Romance* Series

Inadmissible: Love

FOUND: LOVE

•

Donna Wright

AVALON BOOKS
NEW YORK

PRINTED IN THE UNITED STATES OF AMERICA
ON ACID-FREE PAPER
BY HADDON CRAFTSMEN, BLOOMSBURG, PENNSYLVANIA

For Daddy

Every story has another story behind it—this one is no different. There is no way I can ever sufficiently thank the Smoky Mountain Romance Writers for all the support I gather from them. Sharon Griffith, who is the Queen of Tweak. That inner circle of writers, both published and unpublished, who have shown me true friendship, including Holly Jacobs, Debra Webb, Tanya Michaels, and Heather and Terescia. Also Rita Cope; the old gang at FPC, and the gang at Superior; Marlene and Denise, just for being there when I need you. David Popiel and the late Nancy Petrey for giving me my start. Erin Cartwright-Niumata, the greatest editor and friend I could have. My family, Lynn and Ben, who now *really* wonder if I'll ever leave the office. And, of course, my Lord and Savior, Jesus Christ, Who commands all and saw fit for me to realize my dream. Thank you.

Chapter One

"Joey!" Tessa yelled the name of her sister's pet pig in the hopes he'd obey.

Unfortunately, Joey never did as Tessa wanted. The routine, monotonous to say the least, included pigheaded determination to make it to the beautiful flower garden next door.

He had a penchant for Sam Miller's tulips.

Tessa, roped into the role of pig sitter, tired of the game after only three days.

Her sister, Danielle, had "inherited" the little miniature potbellied pig when he became the center of a lawsuit she worked on a few years ago. Now Danni and her husband, Mike, kept the pig and loved him as if he were their child.

1

Joey, however, became angry when they left him behind for vacations and had his own way of handling his resentment. It always included making Tessa's life miserable.

One of those moments loomed before her even now. Her next-door neighbor, an older gentleman, could be quite a grouch. He especially hated to see the little pig root in his flowers.

"This isn't going to work, Joseph Sommers," she muttered, calling Joey by the name her sister used when scolding him. "Mr. Miller already hates you and I can understand why. You have to learn to live in the real world where everything isn't yours."

She picked up Joey as he squealed and wiggled; she hoped to sneak back to her own yard before Mr. Miller saw them. She noticed a car in the man's driveway she hadn't seen before and hoped it wasn't someone with animal control. Mr. Miller threatened to call them for her failure to keep the pig on a leash, or at least in *her* yard.

"The next time your mother goes somewhere," she told the pig as if he could understand, "You'll go with your Uncle Alex. Or your grandparents. I haven't lived in this neighborhood long enough to make enemies."

Her sister and brother-in-law were on a

much needed extended getaway. They'd been married two years, but each enjoyed a successful law career, and this had been the first chance they'd had for a real vacation since their honeymoon.

No sooner had Tessa settled Joey back inside than a knock came on her door. When she opened it, a handsome man stood facing her. Longish dark hair, big blue eyes, and a very confused look. Must be from animal control, she thought.

"May I help you?"

Her friendliness appeared to embarrass him. "Do you own a *pig*?"

Busted.

"I don't really *own* a pig, as it were."

"Well, you *did* pick him up from next door and bring him into your house."

Busted times two.

Mr. Miller had seen Joey in his flowers.

"The pig isn't mine. I'm pig sitting."

"Whose pig is it?"

"My sister's." Then, just for good measure she threw out the words, "She's a lawyer." Maybe Mr. Handsome would back off with that information.

Instead he looked even more confused. "The pig is a lawyer?"

"No, my sister's the lawyer." She chuckled. "The pig belongs to her. Anyway, you wouldn't be here if Mr. Miller, the old crank that lives next door, hadn't called you. Right?"

He cleared his throat. "Mr. Miller is my father."

Busted times three. I'm out.

She cringed. "Oh. I'm sure he's only cranky when Joey gets in the flowers."

"Actually," he eased into a smile and Tessa's heart raced, "he's pretty cranky most of the time."

"I *am* sorry about the little guy. He gets mad at my sister when she leaves him. Then he takes it out on me and your dad's flowers."

As Tessa spoke Joey wandered over to the door, ready to make another break for the garden.

Mr. Handsome Miller reached down and scooped him up, held the pig at eye level, and shot him a stern look. "Oh, no you don't. You need to stay inside with Aunt . . . ?" He glanced toward Tessa.

"Tessa. Tessa Price."

He tucked Joey under his arm like a football and smiled. "Brian Miller. Son of Crank."

She opened her door wider. "Why don't you come in and get some cookies to take home to your dad. Maybe they'll cheer him up and he'll forget about those tulips."

"Fat chance." He followed her through the doorway, putting Joey on the floor gently. "Dad's place is one of those 'garden spots' featured on Channel Eleven every year."

"Really?"

He sat on a bar stool in her kitchen without being asked. "Oh, yeah. I hear about flowers from March to November."

She opened up a bag of cookies and offered him one. "I haven't been here long enough to really know any of these things. Is that your car in the drive?" The aroma of the oatmeal cookies permeated the room as she popped one in her mouth.

"I just bought this one. I'm not sure I like it, but I thought it was the law that all single men drive an SUV."

Single? I'm more interested each minute.

"I don't know, since I'm not a single man." Her nose involuntarily scrunched, "These smell better than they taste, don't they?"

"Yeah, but I liked the pig, so I didn't say anything." His smile focused on her.

A nice smile, she decided, full of warmth and a little flirty.

"Never fear. I have brownies to share. I'm

in a chocolate mood, anyway. The oatmeal really didn't do the trick."

At that moment, Lilly, Danni's dog, found the energy to enter the kitchen and yawn. She reared on her hind legs and put her front paws on Brian's leg. If Tessa didn't know better, she'd have sworn the dog smiled at him.

He rubbed the dog behind the ears. "Who's this?"

Tessa leaned against the counter. "That would be Lilly, also Danni's. As you've guessed by now, I'm a sucker for petsitting for her."

He regarded her with humor. "You know what I think? I think you like it but won't admit it."

She returned his smile. "I do like the animals, but I don't have a good place to keep them here."

"Why didn't you just stay at your sister's place?"

"I just bought this house and didn't want to leave it."

He took a brownie from the plate she offered. "I can understand that. It would be hard for your family, anyway." His expression urged her to answer the unasked question.

"My family?" She depicted an ease she

didn't really feel. "I'm just an old maid school teacher."

"I can see that." He winked.

"Oh, yeah." Her smile widened, in spite of herself. "My brother is finishing up medical school, so he has reason to be unmarried, but me? I'm just single because I'm so hard to live with."

Joey entered the room, went straight to the door, and scratched.

"Oh, no!" she moaned. "He needs to go out. If I don't let him out immediately, he'll leave me a present." She hurriedly found his leash. "If you want to wait, I'll be back in one second flat."

"Don't worry about it." He threw the award-winning grin her way again.

Joey pulled on the leash. "I'd better get him out of here." She pulled a plastic container from the cabinet. "Fill this up. Take as many brownies as you want."

As she raced out the door she threw over her shoulder, "And, tell your dad I'm working on the garden/pig situation!"

"I'll do that." He held up the plastic box. "Thanks." Following her orders, Brian filled the container. When he finished, he walked out her back door and stepped over the small decorative fence that couldn't keep the determined little pig from his dad's prize garden.

He tried to watch as nonchalantly as he could as she took the pig from place to place, as one would a dog. *She's got it all, from head to toe. Well, everything except how to conquer a pig.*

He opened the back door to his dad's house.

"Well, did you talk to her?" His father waited and pounced as soon as the knob turned.

Brian sighed. "Yes. She's very nice and sent you some brownies."

"Is that all?" His father didn't hide his irritation.

Brian put the container on the table. "She said she was sorry, the pig isn't hers and she'll try to keep him out of your garden while she has him in custody."

Sam Miller sat down at his kitchen table and got a brownie from the container. "Figured she could cook." He licked chocolate brownie icing from his fingertips.

A little dazed and confused from his encounter with the petite golden-haired beauty, Brian asked, "What's that mean?"

"Nothing. I'm glad you got it straightened out about that little varmint. He'll ruin my place on the Garden Spot this year."

"The next time you need to talk to her, you go. I'm not around enough do your dirty work."

"I think it's better when you help, because some people think I'm a little grumpy. I don't want to cause any problems with the neighbors."

Brian almost choked on the brownie he munched. "Grumpy? Really? Since when?"

"Since Mrs. Henderson said she'd like to go to dinner with me, only everyone in the neighborhood thought I was a grouch."

"Mrs. Henderson? The woman who's hated me since I was eight and I accidently broke her window with a baseball?"

"I'm sure she's over that by now. I did fix the darn thing."

"And ever since, whenever there was mischief in the neighborhood, she told any victims I was probably the one who did it." He waited a long moment thinking this one out. "I don't know, Dad."

"Before you were ever born, Brian, her husband walked out and all she had left was the house. A person can grow bitter with no family."

"I'll buy that." Brian walked past the table wondering if he should tell his dad the word for him was *crank* instead of *grouch*. He looked out his father's window, from which he could see Tessa's front porch. "Your lady friend is at the "house of pig" even as we speak."

Mrs. Henderson's knock pulled Tessa from her thoughts of Brian Miller.

"Mrs. Henderson. Is everything alright?"

The older woman's voice reminded Tessa of fingernails on a blackboard. "Actually, Tessa, I need some advice and thought you'd be the best person to help me."

Tessa backed away from the door to let the older woman in the house. She had to be a lonely person, totally harmless in the grand scheme of things.

"Let me put Joey on his leash and tie him in the yard so I can give you my undivided attention."

After she finished her chore she sat down on the couch opposite the other woman. "Now, what can I do for you?"

Mrs. Henderson appeared nervous, straightening her already perfectly coiffed gray hair. "Was Brian Miller here?"

"Yes. Joey's been in Mr. Miller's flowers again."

"Just as I thought. You be careful of Brian."

"*Really?*" Tessa wanted to hear more about the guy. Maybe he wasn't so nice. Maybe he wasn't charming and sweet. Maybe—but she'd have to hear this out before she made a decision.

"He's been trouble since he was a child. Loud didn't even begin to describe him. And, no matter what he did, he could talk his way out of it. Not just with his family, either. Every time I called the police on him and his friends, he found a way out of it."

"You called the police? Why?"

"Once, my yard was toilet papered. I know he and his friends did it, but I couldn't prove it. No one ever listened to me. His parents said he was with them at a ball game. But, I know he had something to do with it."

"I'm sure his father wouldn't lie, Mrs. Henderson."

"His father? Nothing but a womanizer. He asked me to go to dinner. As if I need a man to help me eat." She continued to ramble gossip not only about the Millers, but everyone on the block.

Tessa tried to get out of the conversation. "I haven't been home from work long—"

"Another thing about Brian. He can't hang on to a job. He goes from place to place to place, just begging for work. No one knows what he really does. I think he may be into, well, you know."

First Tessa nodded then shook her head. "No, I don't."

"Sure, you do."

"No really, I don't."

The older woman whispered as if someone might hear her, "Something bad."

"I don't think I understand."

"Of course you wouldn't, a nice girl like you." She patted Tessa's leg.

"My dad's a cop. I know about bad things."

Mrs. Henderson talked to Tessa with a note of condescension in her voice. "Whatever it is, I'm sure that he's up to no good. You just have to know him, Tessa."

Uncomfortable with the turn the conversation took, Tessa didn't comment further and was glad when Mrs. Henderson offered to leave.

"I have to be going. Is there anything I can do to help you this evening, Hon?"

"No, not at all, Mrs. Henderson. But, it's always nice when you stop by."

"Well, dear, you know I'd be glad to help you any way I can."

"I really appreciate it, but I need to get Joey back inside."

"Oh, my! You don't need to keep that thing in the house."

Tessa tried to keep the anger from her voice. "Mrs. Henderson, I really need to get some things done before I work on lesson plans, so if you'll excuse me."

"You just remember Brian Miller is no good. He won't work or what he does is bad. On top of all that, that father of his is a gigolo." Mrs. Henderson appeared quite pleased with herself. "I'm so glad to be able to tell you these things before he turns on the charm and you start to like him."

After she said a real good-bye to Mrs. Henderson, Tessa ushered her out of the house. She wasn't surprised when, instead of going home, Mrs. Henderson went next door.

She mulled over Mrs. Henderson's gossip. Sounded to her like Brian had quite a normal childhood.

Tessa had no ambition to work on lesson plans so late in the year. Instead, she gathered her animals and went through her usual evening responsibilities, including nuking and eating a low-fat, cardboard dinner. She couldn't help but think of Brian Miller. But just because she was almost twenty-seven and appeared destined for spinsterhood didn't mean every good-looking guy who walked in her house was fair game.

Sure it did, came the answer from her inner mind. But, she wanted more stability than a roving-a roving, whatever the occupation might be.

Relaxed on her couch, she looked at her nemesis. "*You,* little guy, are going to have to stay out of Mr. Miller's flowers. Okay?"

Joey laid down at her feet, but Tessa wasn't easily fooled. The motion was not one of compliance. No, he'd do as he darned well pleased with her trailing behind him to clean up the mess.

She heard Brian's car start and drive away. "Of course, if the SUV is parked in the driveway, I may beat you to Mr. Miller's flowers."

Joey looked at her and snorted.

That night she sat outside and watched all the lights go out in the neighborhood. One of the things Tessa loved about having her own home was her front porch. Sometimes, she'd even forgo the seat and sit on the steps as she looked into the sky, amazed at the vastness of the universe.

Tonight was a step night versus a seat night.

She didn't feel small as she gazed into the heavens; in fact, it often gave her strength to think so much didn't depend on her. It all ran itself. Contentment coursed through her like a warm drink on a cold night.

Behind her, Joey snorted and grunted. Secured by the loop of his leash around a chair leg, she allowed him to enjoy the cool night air.

She leaned her elbows against the wooden step behind her and sighed. "All is well with the world of Tessa Price."

The words were no more out of her mouth when Joey raced by her in a pink flash. Wood and concrete clicked under his little hooves.

In surprise, Tessa yelled his name. Jumping from her place on the steps she ran after him. From the corner of her eye she saw Brian join in the chase.

Tessa resented the gleam in Joey's eyes as he looked over his shoulder and ran down the sidewalk.

With a flying leap over a hedge and two-stepping around a bicycle, Brian almost had him, but the pig turned the corner of the block.

Tessa grunted. *I'll never pig sit again.* He didn't run fast, but his footwork was impeccable.

Just when she thought he'd run into the street, a particular patch of pansies caught his eye, and Joey stopped to munch.

Out of breath, Tessa and Brian both doubled over, taking in deep gulps of air.

Brian picked up Joey's leash and handed it to Tessa.

She panted the words, "Thank . . . you."

He straightened and waved his hand. "Glad . . . to help."

They walked back to Tessa's without words, still in recovery from the run.

After she settled Joey inside, she returned to the porch where Brian waited.

He tipped a make believe hat and sounded like a B-western movie hero when he spoke, "You've got yourself a quick little pig there, Miss Tessa."

She answered in the same vein. "Yes, sir, Mr. Miller, we're very proud of his speed."

"Joking aside, Tess, how did he get away this time?"

"I have no idea." She gestured toward the chair in which she sat. "I had his leash under this chair leg. The chair hasn't moved, but he got loose."

A trace of laughter still in his voice, he cocked his head to one side. "You have to give him credit, Tessa. He's smart."

"Yeah. Too smart. Maybe Danni should send him to school . . . in Europe."

A chuckle escaped Brian's lips. "There's a

thought. You could tell everyone you have a nephew who's an Oxford graduate."

A quiet moment passed as her eyes became accustomed to the darkness and could make out his handsome features. Brian looked pensive.

Tessa broke the silence. "A dollar for your thoughts."

He arched a brow.

"Inflation." She shrugged.

"I think you look beautiful in the moonlight."

Warmth flooded her cheeks. "That's only because it's not a bright light. In my bathroom mirror, it gets downright scary at times."

"I can't believe that." He reached forward and pushed a strand of hair behind her ear.

Butterflies swarmed through her stomach as she searched for a change of subject. "Tell me about Brian Miller."

He cleared his throat. "I have a great but sometimes grumpy dad. My mom passed away about four years ago—sudden heart attack. She was amazing. Dad misses her a lot." He paused. "My sister, Emily, lives in Clifton and is vice president of a bank there."

"What do you do?"

"I just go from place to place, making people happy."

"That sounds interesting. Share your secret."

"Lots of talking and tap dancing."

"What does that mean, exactly?"

"I'm out of town most of the time. No time for anything. I sometimes wish I hadn't gotten the traveling bug in my system, but, now that I do, I can't see myself doing anything else."

"I know what you mean," she murmured, "I feel that way about teaching. But, I still don't know if you dance, sing, or work a chain gang."

"I'm a management consultant with a local firm. We have an office here, and a few across the country. I go into businesses and, with statistics in hand, try to show them a more efficient way to operate." He stood. "I've got to go."

She couldn't help but ask him, "Again?"

"After tonight I may try out for the Olympics."

She also rose from her chair. "Brian, just out of curiosity, where did you come from when all this happened?"

He rolled his eyes. "I had forgotten to water the plants on the other side of the house for my dad. I heard you yell."

She nodded.

"In my dad's house, if you say you'll water the plants, even if it's midnight and you have to drive back from your own place, you *will* water the plants." He looked down at her. "You may want to kennel the little guy over there. He's going to get hurt if you don't do something."

She glanced toward the screen door. "Oh, no. Don't worry, Brian. One little piggy isn't going to triumph over me."

"If you say so. Just be careful, okay?" With those words, he left.

Tessa thought about what he said.

Not about Joey.

About his job.

He loved what he did. He had the traveling bug, and he wouldn't settle down for anything.

Not even a woman with a pig.

Chapter Two

After a busy day of work, Brian arrived at his apartment building the next afternoon to find his new neighbors lowering the property value. They partied, drank, smoked things they shouldn't, and hated Brian because he didn't. Only home a couple of weeks and already he'd had to go upstairs at three A.M. and ask them to turn down the music. They didn't much like it, and, to be honest, Brian knew he didn't give them the best impression either.

He could keep up with his dad's temper when need be.

He occupied the bottom level of the two-story, converted garage and the Warrens lived above.

21

A moving van parked in their part of the drive put Brian in good spirits. *They're moving! Yes!*

He thought about what it would be like to have a pretty neighbor, like Tessa Price, to bake brownies and only bother him occasionally with a pig problem. He could handle that.

But he wouldn't either. His business didn't allow for relationships.

Mr. Warren, tattooed from head to toe, walked down the steps with a large box in hand. He put the box on the back of the truck and turned toward Brian as he got out of his SUV. "You won, Miller. Old man Taylor threw us out."

Brian tried to look sympathetic. "I'm sorry. I haven't called him, if that's what you think."

Warren only glared. "Yeah, right. You know what they say, Miller, I was born at night, but not last night."

"Think what you want." Brian walked away with caution. He wouldn't put it past Warren to attack him from behind. All he heard was the man spit as Brian opened his door and, after entering his own apartment, locked it behind him.

He stayed up for a while, reading. The

whole time he heard the scraping of furniture across the floor and thought maybe he should go help, as a peace offering.

They probably wouldn't appreciate the gesture. He wondered if they'd see it only as a way to get them out faster.

A couple of hours later, he readied for bed, turning off all the lights. By morning, they'd be gone and a dream would be fulfilled—not have to worry about his home when business took him away.

The next morning, Brian went to the local office of the firm where he worked. Most people didn't even understand what a management consultant did, but Brian led the troops of Enhancement Consultants to one of the top spots in the country.

And, he loved his job, even if it did mean traveling and not having a real life. He shook off those thoughts.

His day, as usual, consisted of lots of meetings and paperwork.

Jim Powell caught him in the hall. "You still here?"

"You make the schedule, big guy. I'd rather be in London on a day like today."

"London. Isn't that where you met that cute computer analyst?"

"Yep." His smile didn't reveal his thoughts were on a pretty blond teacher and not the English "bird" he'd met a few months ago.

"Come on in my office; I want to ask you something."

Brian followed Jim and sat down in an overstuffed leather chair across from his supervisor.

"Sherry and I have been talking." Jim picked up a pencil, but Brian noticed it was more to fidget with than use.

"Okay. Is that good or bad?" Brian didn't let either Sherry or Jim scare him. He knew his position was secured by his reputation.

"She thinks you may be getting burnt out."

Incredulous, Brian asked, "Why would that even enter her mind? I promised her when I wanted off the road, I'd ask."

"Oh, I know." He knew the next words out of Jim's mouth would be a lie. "I just wanted you to know that the Seattle and Detroit offices have openings for a top guy. You could have either office if you wanted it."

Oh. I get it now. "Look, Jim. I'm not coming off the road right now. So, if someone thinks I'm after a job here, I'm not."

Jim appeared to relax at his words. "Good to hear. When you go in and lay the groundwork in a company, it's always the best.

Anyway, you have no reason to hang around. You're not an old married man, like me."

"Nope. Not married and not staying in town for any length of time."

Brian stood with Jim following suit. "I need to go, Jim. I've got paperwork to do."

The next ten hours were filled with monotonous but necessary paperwork and he looked forward to a peaceful evening at home, in front of the television with a cold drink. Or maybe a trip to see his dad, to check up on him and his garden, of course.

He loosened his tie as he pulled into the drive of his apartment. Maybe he should just buy a house. He'd lived in this apartment for some time now and every time someone new moved in upstairs they were always worse than the last.

Of course, buying a home would mean doing some yard work and other upkeep. And, he wasn't sure he could stand being in one place all the time; after all, he'd been on the road for five years.

He got out of his car and inserted the key in his door lock. The sight that greeted him left him agape. He no longer had a choice of moving. His apartment, ruined by vandals, looked ravaged by war. He had no words to describe his fury.

* * *

Joey did his best to get to Mr. Miller's flowers before Tess could pull his leash and get him under control. They played tug-of-war for a few minutes, then Joey gave in to Tess. If she didn't know better, she'd think the little fellow grinned at her as if she met his expectations.

She couldn't help but notice Brian's car parked not too far from Mr. Miller's garage. *Hmmm. Still there from yesterday.* The vehicle overflowed with what looked to be all of someone's possessions. Boxes and bags of clothing, books, papers, and even a coffee maker piqued her interest more than she wanted to admit. She wondered if Mr. Miller was moving out, or Brian was moving in.

She didn't stop more than to check the mailbox, because it would make her appear anxious to see him. Not that she wouldn't like to see him, but he didn't need to know it.

Back inside, she assured herself Lilly and Joey were sleeping soundly, then found a used dryer sheet in the utility room to dust off her computer and television screens.

The doorbell rang.

Brian.

She quickly straightened herself in the downstairs bathroom mirror and went to the door. Taking a deep breath, she opened it.

Mrs. Henderson rushed inside, passing Tess as if she weren't there. "Have you heard?"

Tess closed the door. "Heard what?"

"Why, that Brian Miller has been at it again. Do you have any tea, dear?"

Tessa's mind raced to Brian, but she had to address Mrs. Henderson's question before she got her answers. "I always do my cleaning on Saturdays, Mrs. Henderson. I don't have anything to offer you, I'm sorry."

Mrs. Henderson sat down in the old easy chair Tessa had inherited from her grandmother. "That's alright, dear. In my day, a woman always had something on hand, but this *is* a different generation."

Get on with your story. "You were about to tell me something?"

"Oh my, yes! That Brian Miller got into an awful fistfight with his neighbor and had to be asked to leave his apartment. He's moving in with his father for a few weeks, until he can find something. I knew from the moment he turned nine and his baseball came through my window he'd turn out no good. I told Mr. Johnson that I doubt Brian can afford anything else with his work habits."

Tessa stiffened with annoyance. Brian's work may be different, but apparently he made a living.

"My word!"

Joey sniffed the older woman's ankles.

Mrs. Henderson almost jumped on a chair. "You've let that thing in here again!"

Tessa pulled Joey toward her, scratching him behind the ears. "He's like a puppy, Mrs. Henderson. He won't hurt you."

"I'm sorry, I just don't abide farm animals in the house. I'm going to have to leave." She marched to the door, but turned to Tessa. "Just remember, stay away from that Miller boy. He's nothing but trouble and that's all he's ever been."

As Tessa returned to her cleaning, she resented the woman's words regarding Joey. Maybe he was a little pig, but he was house broken. Usually. When Tessa didn't keep him.

As far as Brian was concerned, his work may not be conventional, but he paid his bills, at least as far as Tessa knew. He drove a brand new SUV. That meant he paid at least one. And, to hold it against him that his baseball hit her window when he was nine? Mrs. Henderson wouldn't have survived in Tessa's childhood neighborhood, not with her brother Alex and his affinity for the sport. He broke two different windows out of their house.

No, Mrs. Henderson wasn't the sweet little old lady type that Tessa had first thought her to be. She'd already discussed Brian's situation with someone else on the block. The woman gossiped. Not just little rumors, either, but malicious stories that could ruin a person's reputation. She knew enough about men to know he may not be the perfect gentleman he appeared to be. But, she also knew Mrs. Henderson's word didn't hold water with her. Not after this evening.

As his father went from window to window looking for God knew what, Brian put together a sandwich.

"Dad," Brian asked between bites, "Why don't you fix me fancy Sunday dinners?"

His father faced him. "Why couldn't you have been a sweet girl who'd take care of her elderly father?"

"Want a sandwich?"

The older man shrugged. "Why not?"

Brian teased him. "You still want to get *cozy* with Mrs. Henderson?"

"Hmph. That woman. I don't know what I was thinking. But, whatever it was, I'm not thinking it anymore. You want some milk?"

"Sure."

His father began his usual tirade while pouring the milk. "I was thinking, son. You have no kids, no responsibility. A job that takes you all over the world. Used to be, a man of thirty-two was thought to be just a *little* strange if he wasn't married by your age."

Brian took a drink of his milk and put the glass down. "Dad, in this day and age, people don't marry until they're older, settled, and can afford it."

"Hogwash!" His father disagreed. "No one is ever old enough, settled enough, or can afford to get married. There's something wrong with the young people today." He took a bite of the cold chicken sandwich.

"Don't get mad at me. I think it's when I introduce my dates to you that they take off."

"Shush!" His father said.

Brian didn't say a word. Just stopped in mid-bite.

"I can hear that pig at it again."

Brian put down his food and walked outside.

Joey rooted at a small tree in Tessa's yard. Around the tree a good-sized rope restrained him. Brian didn't have to go into her yard to see the security, now turned up a notch, should do the trick.

Disappointment flooded him and he knew why. With this false alarm he had no excuse to see the pretty lady next door.

He returned to the kitchen. "Joey is in Tessa's yard, not yours."

"So you didn't talk to her?"

"Did you expect me to?" He changed the subject. "I'm hungry. I thought I'd finish supper before I went anywhere, if you don't mind." He took a big bite of his sandwich to keep his father's inquiries at bay. He couldn't answer with his mouth full.

"She's an awfully pretty little thing, you know."

Brian took a drink of milk to wash down a mouthful of sandwich. "I know what the woman looks like. She's very attractive, but where would I put her, in my suitcase? I love what I do, Dad. I've seen parts of the world most people only dream of."

A moment of awkward silence followed Brian's speech. "Even if I wanted to settle down, there's no place in this office for me. I'd have to move to Detroit, so what difference would it make?"

"But, you have thought about it?" His dad sat down across from him.

Brian paused a moment. "Yeah." His words surprised even him. "I have thought about it."

Sam's eyes twinkled. "Why do you think you're suddenly thinking about it?"

Brian didn't answer. He took another bite and ignored the question altogether. He knew the answer. In fact, they both knew what it was. Or, rather, who.

His father took a drink of his milk and changed the subject, which met Brian's approval. "What did your landlord say about your things?"

Brian swallowed. "The Warrens left no forwarding address. The upstairs is empty, but looks worse than my place—if that's possible. The graffiti isn't fit for the human eye." Brian shook his head. "In my place, if it was electrical, they soaked it in water. If it was clothing, they spray painted. Mr. Taylor just told me he doesn't have insurance against vandalism."

Brian slapped a hand on the table. "Almost everything I own is ruined. But, Taylor found no reason for that type of insurance. After all, it was a garage, what could anyone do to the outside? He didn't think about anyone damaging the inside."

His father nodded in agreement. "Does he know how they got in?"

"That's what really makes me angry." Brian picked up his milk and took a drink. "He admitted the same keys fit both apartments."

"I'm sorry, son. But, with all the security deposits and credit checks, you'd think the Warrens could be traced."

"If this guy had used his own information,

we'd be fine. According to Mr. Taylor, the police picked up Mr. Warren at work and it turned out to be his brother, who now also has a warrant out on the guy."

His father shook his head. "When are you supposed to leave for your next job?"

"*There's* more good news. I thought I'd just put my stuff in storage. What I have left, I should say. I don't have another assignment lined up for the next six weeks."

His father brightened. "I hope you know you're staying right here with me. Just think, we can get together with your sister and her family and I can have all of you here at one time."

Sam's eager expression told Brian to cancel the hotel reservation he'd already made. "Are you sure it's okay?"

He slapped Brian's shoulder. "I'm excited to have you home, son."

With forced enthusiasm Brian patted his father's arm. "Great. I'll stay here."

Chapter Three

Tessa's day, finally over—thank God—couldn't get any worse. No way. If she picked it up, she dropped it. If she said it, her foot landed in her mouth. One thing didn't make the day bad; everything did. In the classroom, the teacher's lounge, even the principal's office, nothing went right.

When she got home, she noted no SUV.

Good, no one should see her in this mood. She needed to relax in a bath full of lavender bubbles.

And, pig or no pig, that's what she planned to do. Joey lounged in his favorite chair when she opened the door and went inside. Lilly looked at her from the couch. After she took both of them outside for a short walk, she returned them to their nap areas and went upstairs to run her bath.

When she came downstairs, Joey stood at the front door, sniffing. His curly tail wagged. "Oh, no you don't, little man. Not this evening. I'm not running after you."

A knock came on the door.

When she opened it, Brian stood before her, a bundle of flowers in his hand. "My dad asked me to bring these over as a thank-you for doing so well at keeping your pig from his prize petunias."

"I didn't know your father had petunias."

"He doesn't." He leaned against the door jam. "Just a little alliteration."

How could she contain the smile that pulled at her mouth?

Brian, dressed in a suit as if he'd just gotten off work, made her jeans and shirt that had definitely seen better days feel out of place.

"These roses are gorgeous. This peachy color is so unusual." She looked from the flowers to Brian, "You're welcome to stay for dinner, just let me get the animals out—"

The phone rang. She eyed it and the animals.

He smiled and offered to help, "I'll put Joey and Lilly out; you get your phone."

Outside, he tied Lilly to her stake and Joey around the tree to which he found him tied the other day.

Back inside, he found Tessa looking at the phone, though not talking on it.

"Are you telepathically speaking to someone?"

A sheepish look crossed her face. "Kind of."

Brian waited for an explanation.

"It's April."

He sat down at the bar. The silence as she stared at the phone became interminable.

"Tessa, do you have something to tell me, or do I need to do some kind of psychic thing?"

"That was my mom. Every April I have to come up with a reason I can't participate in the Literacy Auction in June."

"And, why can't you?"

"That's just it. I don't have an excuse this year."

"Then do it."

"Do you know what's involved?" she asked as she began taking the makings of a salad from the fridge.

He pulled a piece of lettuce from the pile and munched it. "No, I don't think I do."

"The person being auctioned stands in front of all kinds of people, normally the local Bar

Association, and holds a sign for a service or place of business. Then, one of the judges auctions off the dinner, or motorcycle ride, or whatever, and you go with the highest bidder to the dinner or on the ride."

"I get the picture. Doesn't sound so bad to me."

She sliced a tomato. "My sister Danni went for fifteen hundred dollars. Her now-husband wanted a chance to meet her."

"What did you go for?"

"I didn't. I begged out the last two years. But, this year Mother isn't taking no for an answer."

She paused. "Okay, deep breath." She took one. "Subject change. How was your day?"

"Not bad. I've had better. My supervisor let me know that there were open jobs in the company where I wouldn't be traveling so much."

Tessa's heart jumped. He'd be here in town? Her day just got better.

"But, none in Fort White, of course. Because that would be his job."

Her heart sank.

She tried to sound indifferent. "But, would you want to come off the road?"

He looked right at her. "I might. If there were a good reason."

This conversation definitely put her heart on a roller coaster. "What kind of reason were you in the market for?" She put the knife down and walked toward the cupboard where she kept her bowls.

He followed her. When she turned back around she was nose to chest with him.

"I thought about a woman who smells like lavender. I like lavender."

She gulped. "Me too."

He took the bowl from her, laid it on the counter, and took her in his arms. "I've noticed that." He nuzzled her neck. "You smell so good, I can't seem to get your fragrance out of my head."

"Brian, you . . ." her voice trailed. What was she going to say, anyway?

"Do you know how beautiful you are?" The words whispered against her ear sent her into a shiver. He seemed to have a power over her.

Brian's pager sounded. He muttered as he stepped back and checked the number. Dialing his cell phone he walked toward her living room. "I'll be back in a second." He winked at her. "Hold my spot, will you?"

She continued to make dinner but, with her living room only a few feet away from where she stood, she couldn't help listening intently to his side of the conversation.

"You're telling me you couldn't make this decision, Jim? I'm in the middle of something. I do have a life, you know." He paused while he listened to the caller. Anger evident in his tone, Brian asked, "Didn't you tell Sherry?"

Again, he waited on an answer. "I think not. She needs to be made aware of this situation. If this were a new client, I wouldn't say that, but they've been with us since before the Dead Sea was sick. No. You let Sherry decide this one, that is, if you can't."

He snapped his phone shut and stood near her stairway. As if studying a place on her wall, he stood perfectly still.

Finally, she became uncomfortable enough to interrupt his thoughts. "You okay?"

"It's work." He turned around and walked to her, taking her into his arms again, allowing his lips to settle on her forehead. "I need to go. I have something I need to do."

She tried to hide her disappointment as she slid her arms around his shoulders. "That's fine. I haven't put the steaks on yet, anyway."

He kissed her gently. Warm and sweet. "Will you go out with me tomorrow night?"

How could she say no. "Of course." Her words sounded raspy in her ears.

"I'll call you by five." He left after another kiss.

It had been some time since she'd had a real relationship. She wondered if she could even do this.

Her fingers trailed her lips where he'd kissed her. She would certainly give it a try.

The small, quiet restaurant gave Tessa a deep feeling of contentment. No students. No colleagues. No dogs. No pigs. Just her and a Greek salad made in heaven.

Sitting across from Brian Miller didn't hurt the situation in the least. Now that he'd shown an obvious interest, however, she felt a little shy.

He crossed his arms in front of him on the table and leaned forward. "Tell me about your life, Tessa. Tell me everything."

She put her fork down and stared into those big blue eyes. "I'm the youngest of three children. My parents are retired. Dad was a cop; Mom a schoolteacher. My sister is an attorney, who hates the term 'ambulance chaser,' and my brother just passed his boards and is an urgent care doctor. And, he hates the term 'quack,' but that doesn't stop me from using either. And, you?" She took a drink of her water.

"Okay. My mom stayed home and dad was a construction foreman. I spend most of my time on the road."

She leaned back in her chair as the waiter refilled their water glasses. "What exactly is it that you do?"

"I'm a management consultant with one of the larger firms downtown. Ever heard of Enhancement Consultants?"

She shook her head.

"Most people haven't. But we're world-wide. I go from company to company auditing their books, procedures, anything they do. Then, I tell them how they can do it better."

"That's certainly different. There's really a call for that kind of thing? All over the world?"

"Sure." An idea sprang to his mind. "Think of it this way. You have a pig that is, to say the least, out of control at times. I would come in and show you how to handle him with the lowest amount of fallout for your company."

Her countenance changed as she began to eat again. "Joey is *not* out of control. He's just reacting to Danni and Michael leaving town."

"That's the attitude most people have when they see me coming. Why should anyone need a consultant? But, believe me, you could use a consultant, just like most companies."

Tessa abruptly put down her fork, wiped her mouth with her napkin, and sat back in her chair. "Are you saying you can handle Joey better than I can?"

"What I meant was—"

"What you *said* was I needed a consultant to handle one little pig. Is that what you think or not? If it is, at least admit it."

He cleared his throat. *One Greek salad: wasted.* "I think you could use some help with him, yes. That doesn't mean you aren't a capable person."

Pursing her lips, she nodded. "I see."

The waiter approached. "Would you like dessert?"

"I would." Tessa looked at Brian with a gleam in her eye and ordered. "I'll have a chocolate fudge sundae, with nuts, extra whipped cream, and two cherries."

"And, for you, sir?"

"I think I'll have the same, and a cup of decaf."

The waiter withdrew to place their order.

"I'll tell you what, Mr. Traveling Troublemaker. I'll let you walk Joey on Saturday. By the time you get back, you'll be glad to go back to your father and his tulips. And, if you're not, I'll—" She stopped talking as she thought. "Oh! I know. I'll make you dinner."

An easy way out. "Sounds good. That way you can do anything you need without worrying about him for an hour or so." He sipped his water. "And, I'll forget the Traveling Troublemaker comment."

With a smug look she told him, "No need on my account."

The remainder of the evening went very well. They laughed and joked until they got to Tessa's door, and that awkward moment of "should we–or–shouldn't we?" kiss good night bloomed in full.

Brian took matters into his own hands. First, he took her hand, then touched her cheek. A sweet kiss followed. Longer than Tessa expected, but welcome all the same. The warmth and firmness of his mouth made her want to melt into him. Instead, when he pulled away slightly, she tried to become rational again.

He mumbled, "Is this lip gloss strawberry?"

"Uh, huh." The answer came from an incoherent state of mind.

"I really like strawberries." Another kiss, and he pulled away. "I'll call you tomorrow." She could get used to his handsome grin among other things.

* * *

The next day, a bright, beautiful Friday morning, seemed like a great day to take Joey to school. Tessa's fourth graders thought Joey should wear a crown and be king.

As spoiled as the pet was, he enjoyed all the attention. This worked out extremely well, and she wondered if maybe this was what she should do with him until her sister came home.

Katie, the other fourth grade teacher, met Tessa in the schoolyard. They usually sat together at recess and the day was too beautiful to pass up.

"Who is *this?*" Katie asked as she plopped down on the wooden bench.

"This is Joey." Tessa smiled, as much from the sun in her eyes as a welcome to her friend.

"The famous pig?"

"This is the one."

Joey snorted and moved up against Katie's leg as any dog or cat would to be petted.

Katie obliged him. "He's so sweet."

"He can be. And, he can be murder. The couple that had him before Danni and Mike spoiled him rotten. At least Danni doesn't dress him up."

Laughter poured from her friend. "You must be kidding? They dressed him up?"

"I promise. Big Tennessee University fans;

they put him in blue sweaters and jeans. Even little caps with places cut out for his ears." She motioned with her fingers near her ears to make her point.

"I remember the Fairmont Farms people used him as a part of their ads. Why didn't they keep him after they divorced? I forgot that part."

Tessa grinned slyly. "That part never made it into the papers. The ads lost their popularity after the court battle over his custody was flaunted all over the media. The couple settled and neither wanted him."

"Embarrassing what people will do to each other."

They remained quiet a moment.

Katie broke the silence. "He's well behaved at least."

"Ha!" Tessa scoffed. "You've been petting his head since you sat down. As long as I give him my attention every waking moment, he's fine. But, he really hates it when Danni leaves and shows it by running from me every chance he gets."

"Why not just kennel him?"

"Don't ever let my sister hear you say that. She'd take the vapors and swoon."

"I take it she's attached to him?"

"She has the sweetest dog, just wants love and food, but the pig . . . let's just say he's trying my patience. He's learned how to dig up the stake I tie him to in my yard."

"I didn't realize they were so smart."

"After he gets away, he runs to the neighbor's house to root up his prize winning garden."

"I'll bet he's making friends for you in your new place."

Tessa couldn't help but think of Brian. "You could say that."

"Meaning?"

"The man next door has a son. He found Joey in his dad's flowers."

"Do you have a crush on the boy next door?"

"Oh, that's a story in itself." Tessa told her about the date, emphasizing how Brian explained his occupation. "Other than that, we had a really good time."

"No good night kiss, huh?"

Tessa's mood changed. His good night kiss had kept her awake most of the night. "I don't want to talk about it."

"You're blushing, Miss Price."

"I also made him a bet." She told Katie to get her off the subject of Brian as an object of affection. "If he can take Joey on a walk without the pig running him all over the walking track, I'll treat him to dinner."

Katie laughed. "What do *you* get if *you* win?"

"A chance to say I told you so. And, that's good enough."

"Men," Katie said, "Can't live without them. Can't live with them."

"You're married, so I guess you *can* live with them."

Katie shrugged. "Don't count on it."

Concern inundated Tessa. "What's that supposed to mean?"

"It means even those of us in wedded bliss can't live with them, sometimes."

Tessa became concerned. "Is everything alright?"

"Sure. Paul will be out of the dog house as soon as he grovels at my feet."

"Should all men learn to grovel, Oh Married One?"

"Absolutely!" She shrugged matter-of-factly. "The way things are, I expect flowers today or tomorrow."

Tessa bit her lip to stifle a grin.

Glad that nothing too bad nipped at Katie's marriage, Tessa called her students in from recess.

An hour or so later, Tessa heard the "oohs" and "ahs" from Katie's classroom. She'd loaned her Joey so her children wouldn't miss out on petting the big ham.

After school, she piled him into her car, not without a trial scramble, and took the shortest route home, stopping for nothing.

She got Joey inside and when she took Lilly out to the backyard noticed a particular SUV in Mr. Miller's driveway.

She wondered if his business were lagging since it was only three-thirty and he was already visiting his father.

Lilly barked at a squirrel.

"That's it girl!" Tessa encouraged the dog as she tied her to her stake, "Keep protecting your Aunt Tessa from all those mean, nut-eating animals!"

Lilly looked pleased with herself and Tessa couldn't help but walk to the dog and give her a good belly rub.

Brian soon joined her in the backyard. She shied from him after last night. But, he still had to learn the piggy lesson and his grin told her he thought he was up for the challenge.

"I've been working out, so you don't have to worry about me losing your sister's pig tomorrow."

"I'll tell you what. I've got a couple of steaks that says you can't take him to the track tonight and keep him under control."

Brian cocked his head. "You look so confident. Did you give him some kind of upper pill or vitamin or something?"

"I don't have to."

"Are you going with us?" Brian gestured for her to precede him.

"Of course. How else will I judge how you deal with him?"

She went inside and got the animals' leashes. Upon her return, she found Joey already waiting for her in Brian's car. Tessa leashed Lilly and took her to the car, settling her in the back seat beside the pig.

Brian looked over at her and smiled.

Tessa didn't like the situation, but only said, "I always take Lilly too. This way they both get their exercise."

Brian turned the key. "No problem here."

The running track where she walked the animals was only a few blocks away. On the way there, Joey did every kind of wiggle, tug, and pull imaginable as she tried to put his leash on him.

Finally, she sighed and turned back to the front seat. "You need to do it all, anyway. I'll relax and spend the time with Lilly and you and Joey can . . . well, have fun."

He appeared unruffled. "Fine by me."

After the car stopped, Brian got out and put the leash on Joey. They walked around the track a few times, passing Lilly with Tessa holding the dog's leash.

When Tessa finished the last lap, three women she didn't know stood along side Brian and Joey.

They all cooed over the pig while Brian stood beside him. He awarded them his million-dollar smile as he ate up the attention he and the pig garnered.

The women all dressed in shorts, spandex, or little more than bathing suits. They vied for attention, but not from Joey.

She could hear them from where she strolled.

"Oh, Brian." The blond held onto his arm. "Why don't you take my number?"

The brunette would not be out done. "I'm having a party tomorrow night. Would you like to come?"

Tessa waved at Brian as she and Lilly walked to the car. After a few moments, Brian and Joey met them there.

He grinned. "I think you owe me a steak dinner."

She looked over her shoulder at Joey as she spoke. "Would you prefer ham?"

Brian started the car and pulled away from the park.

I don't believe it. Tessa repeated the words over and over to herself on the way home. "He didn't even try to get away?"

"No. He acted like a perfect little porker."

"I don't believe it."

"Tessa, I could give you a whole lot of grief right now. And, believe me, I'm more than just a little tempted to do just that. But, I think Joey tests limits with you."

"You're telling me. But, he helped you, didn't he? How many phone numbers did you get?"

"I didn't take any numbers."

He pulled the SUV back into the drive. "When your sister—what's her name?"

"Danni."

"Right, Danni. When she's at home, how does he treat you?"

"Just fine."

"He's angry with Danni and you get the brunt of it. Like I said at dinner last night, everyone can use a consultant for one thing or the other."

Brian proved his point and felt better about

the whole situation. "How about if we just grab a burger somewhere?"

"Oh, no. If you were promised dinner, you will get dinner."

Brian took a sidelong glance, not sure of the safety of the situation. "Do you have arsenic?"

"Stay and find out." She got out of the car, but with the window rolled down, she leaned inside, eyes wide. "If you dare."

Chapter Four

Tessa loved Saturdays. It meant she could play in the yard. Flowers, vines, veggies, and animals were all a part of that. She used the morning to plant and the afternoon to rest. No television show could compare to the bathtub and a good book.

After a long, luxurious bubble-filled tub and a mystery that just started to get good as Tessa began to wrinkle, she dressed and took the book downstairs with her.

Mrs. Henderson was at her door with an offer of homemade jelly.

Tessa held the jar in her hand as she opened the door wider to let the woman in. "This is so nice, thank you."

"Oh, I can't come in, Tessa. Just wanted you to have a little something. The block seems so much brighter since you came here."

"That's so sweet, thank you."

"That Brian hasn't been over here bothering you, has he?"

"I wouldn't say that. In fact, he helped me chase down Joey the other night." As an afterthought, she added, "He's a consultant and travels a lot."

"Really?" Mrs. Henderson didn't hide her displeasure. Tessa thought knowing the man had a real job should set the older woman at ease.

"Yes. From what I can see, he does well."

"Isn't that just so nice?" Mrs. Henderson cooed. Or hissed; Tessa wasn't sure which.

Tessa decided not to beat around the bush anymore. "You know, Mrs. Henderson, if you'd lived in my neighborhood as I grew up, you might have gotten a window or two knocked out by flying baseballs or softballs. That just goes with living in a neighborhood with kids."

"Well, it shouldn't! Children should be in their own yards, or better yet, in their houses reading or something constructive. I never had children of my own, but I can tell you, my children would have never done such things."

"Trust me, they don't sit in corners. And, if they did, that would frighten me."

In an effort to strengthen her argument, Mrs. Henderson continued, "He and his friends used to cut through my yard to the field behind my house to play."

"Did they damage your property? Purposefully, I mean. And when he put the baseball through your window, did he offer to pay for it?"

"Offer? Indeed he did not! I marched him straight to Sam Miller and demanded to be paid for it."

"What happened?"

"Well, um . . . Mr. Miller offered to go buy a window and repair it himself."

"I thought so. Well, I need to go tend to my rent-a-pets."

The older woman smiled, but it didn't reach her eyes. "Good-bye, Tessa."

"Thanks again." Tessa closed the door and took the jelly to the fridge.

Mrs. Henderson's stories were all half-truths. Just enough to make them not a real lie. What did she say about Tessa when she wasn't around? With the woman's dislike of Brian, what could she have the whole block thinking about the man, and him not around to defend himself? She noticed him mowing his dad's grass from her kitchen window.

What was it Mrs. Henderson had said about Brian? He'd been in a fistfight with his neighbor? She didn't believe it for a minute, yet that's probably what at least half the people living within walking distance believed right now. Last night, he and Tessa had a wonderful time eating together and ribbing each other. They played a board game and Brian excused himself before ten o'clock. His engaging kisses were warm, but not pushy. *This is not the type of man to fight. Unless provoked.* But, Brian had no marks on him to make her think he'd been in a squabble.

Tessa found Mrs. Henderson guilty.

She shook her head. Now she had a reason to distrust the woman, and once Tessa's trust was lost, it was gone forever.

Sunday afternoon, Tessa returned from her parents for Sunday lunch and decided to get *it* over with. After putting on a pair of shorts and a heavy tee shirt, she called to the animals, "Bath time at Aunt Tessa's!" She chased the animals outside and corralled them after wrestling both to the ground. Yep. Her life was officially the pits.

Danni had called last night from Paris.

Paris!

Not only had she gotten to go on the vacation of a lifetime, while she was there she'd found out she was pregnant. Good fortune. No jealousy. She loved her sister and Danni earned everything she had.

And, she had it all.

But sometimes Tessa, with a guilty heart, wondered why God didn't spread it around a little more.

Of course, the conversation took on a pet theme as well and Tessa assured Danni her present children were doing fine.

In the backyard, she filled a tub with water and carried warm water from her kitchen to keep Lilly from freezing. The poor dog looked at her with those big brown eyes that pleaded, *Why would you do this to me?*

Brian came out of his back door. "Pet washing?"

"It's part of the Aunt Tessa Vacation Package. Bubble baths with a good flea powder rub down afterward."

"Ooh, I might be interested in that," he joked.

She ignored the statement. "And, afterward, we have premium pig chow or canned dog food, your preference, of course."

"I would expect a choice from such a great resort. You could be a travel agent with that ad."

"No thanks. I'll stick to teaching." She dried Lilly off as they spoke. Lilly enjoyed this part of the complete treatment.

Brian looked around. "Is the Olympic runner next?"

"Yes." She sighed. "I dread it. If you think he can run, you should see him wiggle in the tub."

"I'll be glad to help." She knew Brian was sincere with his offer, but she still didn't want the man to show her up with Joey again. Anyway, some women might come from out of the bushes to see him do it, the way they did at the track.

"That's okay, I'll be fine."

"If you say so." He muttered the words.

"You are implying that I do not know how to give my nephew, the pig, a bath."

"I told you. He pushes you. I'll bet you I could give him a bath with a lot less trouble, just because I'm not you."

"You're on. What's the bet?"

"If I'm wrong, I'll . . ." He paused. "Mow your grass."

"Fair enough, and if he doesn't give you the treatment, I'll . . ." her voice trailed as she looked around for something she could do. "I'll wash your car."

He beamed. "Even if I win, *I'll* wash the car."

Brian called to the animal after the water was an appropriate temperature. "Here, Joey!"

Joey went straight to Brian.

Brian pointed toward the tub. "I'm going to give you a bath, little guy. So, I need you to get into the tub."

Joey obeyed.

Brian took the sponge and pet soap and washed the pig without one bit of resistance.

Tessa stood wide-eyed as she watched what appeared to be a man and his pig having a happy bath time.

Experience told her she'd have been soaked from top to bottom and everything in between.

After Brian made sure he'd been scrubbed from snout to tail, he rinsed Joey off and helped him out of the tub. The look on Tessa's face warned him to be good. Gloating at this moment would get him hurt. He kept a straight face, as if there were nothing wrong with the situation. "Do you care if I tie him to the tree or do you want him inside?"

"The tree is fine, thank you." Her reply was a bit garbled, said through gritted teeth.

"Don't try to get away, Joey. Your Aunt Tessa is in no mood to run, okay?"

Joey looked at Tessa then at Brian. Immediately, he sat down.

Tessa's cheeks flushed with what Brian

knew was anger. "Once again, the pig makes his point."

"If Danni hadn't left, Tessa, he'd treat you like he always does. It's just the separation thing."

"You should be soaked from head to toe. You should be standing here looking like a person soaked from head to toe who hates pigs!"

Brian's beeper sounded. "I'm sorry, I'll have to take a rain check on the car wash."

"Anytime is good with me." Then she muttered under her breath, "I'm always here."

A few days later, Brian turned from preparing his weekly car wash supplies and eyed Tessa, her water hose at the ready.

"Drop the sponge and move away from the car." Tessa pointed the hose at Brian's face.

Brian saw a determination in her eyes like nothing he'd seen before, not even in board rooms where millions of dollars were at stake. "Excuse me, Miss Price, but no one washes my car, but me. Bet or no bet."

"Excuse *me*, Mr. Miller, but Tessa Price never welched on a bet in her life. I don't plan to start now. I *will* wash your car, and it *will* be done right. On second thought, when I'm finished it will make you wish you had me to wash it *all* the time."

He picked up the bucket. "Tessa, I don't

mean to hurt your feelings or anything, but I'm not letting you wash my car. That's final."

She held her ground, hose in hand. "I don't want to do this to you, Brian. Please, don't make me."

"You don't have to prove to me that you can do something well. Okay?"

"Is that what you think? That I'm trying to prove a point?" The hose didn't waiver in her hand.

He moved towards her. "I don't believe you'll do it. I think there's a part of you that understands what I'm saying about my vehicle."

She retreated, step-by-step. "I'm warning you, Brian. I'll do it if I have to."

He grabbed the arm holding the nozzle. When he pointed it, and her hand, upwards, she squeezed the trigger. The water came down around them in a light shower.

First, he grinned. Then, upon seeing her blond hair fall in tendrils around her heart shaped face, and the fullness of her lips, he bent slightly and kissed her. Her warm lips felt sweet beneath his.

As he pulled away he pulled the hose with him, turning off the water.

She stood, staring at him. "You shouldn't have done that out here."

"Nope, but," the need to say something

memorable loomed inside him, "I didn't want to waste the moment."

She looked down the driveway. Brian's gaze followed hers and Mrs. Henderson stood before them, mouth agape. She hurried on when she saw she'd been spotted.

"Tess, I think I just ruined your reputation."

"Mrs. Henderson won't . . ." her voice trailed. "Oh, no. You're right, I *am* busted."

"By the time it gets back to my dad, we'll have done much more than a simple kiss."

"In a driveway that joins our yards and where anyone could see. Won't people give me more credit than that?"

"Maybe. If I weren't involved. People believe her when it comes to me. I can't explain why."

An evident change in her countenance alerted him to beware. "I am going to wash your car. You can watch. You can go inside. You can go to . . ." She swallowed hard. "But, I'm going to wash the thing. Do you understand?"

"Yeah." He'd just shattered the woman's character on the whole block. He wouldn't argue with her anymore. "I'll leave you to it."

Chapter Five

With groceries in hand, Brian got out of his car and waved at the lady who lived next door to his father.

Mrs. Weathers not only did not return the gesture, she sniffed and called him a cad.

With each step he took to go inside, he became more furious. "Mrs. Henderson," he muttered, as he put away the items from his plastic bag. "Dad?"

"In the living room!"

Sam gave him a sidelong glance the minute he sat down on the couch. "You okay?"

"Your woman is at it again."

His father, reclining in his favorite chair, sat

forward a little, as if to take in everything Brian said. "My *woman*? Oh, Frieda Henderson. What'd she say?"

"I have no idea."

"Then how do you know she said anything?"

"Because Mrs. Weathers just called me a cad. Anyway, Dad, look at the history. Mrs. Henderson has hated me ever since the window incident."

"When I repaired her window? That doesn't make sense. Just kids playing. Could've happened anywhere."

"Tell *her* that."

Exasperation slowly poured through him. Not only did that woman go around the block saying heinous things about him, but now she'd started on Tessa. Fury waged a war inside him as he contemplated the situation.

Eventually Brian relaxed again. The show they watched in silence had almost caught his attention when he heard a car start next door.

He sat up and looked out the window. Tessa left in her little white late model Chevy. "A little late for Tessa to be leaving the house, wouldn't you say?"

"I don't know, Son. It's only seven. She may need some milk or something."

"I hope nothing's wrong."

"Maybe she's out of whatever it is she feeds that darned pig of hers."

"I told you it's not hers. It's her sister's."

"Yeah, yeah. It still doesn't stay out of my flowers."

"That didn't stop you from sending me to her house with a bunch of roses as a thank you for keeping him out of your pansies."

"Oh, yeah."

"It's called 'selective memory.' I can have you committed in a heart beat." Brian snapped his fingers.

His dad sat back in his easy chair, grinning. "Then what would Mrs. Henderson say?"

Brian sighed. He should've asked Tessa out for tonight. But, instead, he'd decided to play it cool. He didn't want to fall in love and then leave town. He especially didn't want her to get hurt. It was bad enough he'd leave her with Mrs. Henderson's gossip, let alone with a broken heart. He just wouldn't do it.

Upstairs, Brian got ready for bed. *What is wrong with me?* He picked up his pillow and slammed it down on the bed. "I am not falling for Tessa Price."

"Sure you are." Came an answer from the hallway.

"Have you stooped to eavesdropping?"

"I just walked by and heard what you said. You're talking to yourself, by the way. Maybe I should have *you* committed."

Brian walked the few steps to the door and pulled it the rest of the way open to confront his father. "I'm not crazy, and I'm not going to give up my position for the girl next door."

"The first part, probably not. The second, unless you have the guts, then I'd say you're right."

I hate it when he's right. " 'Night Dad."

"Good night, Brian." His father hesitated, then said, "You know. You have to think of what your traveling is worth, Brian. Jobs, heck, with your education and work ethic, they're a dime a dozen. But, a beautiful blond with a pig? Well, let's just say that's not a chance a man gets every day."

Brian tried to read in bed, but all he thought about were his father's words.

It was true; Brian needed to find a way to reconcile this situation between his job and a real life.

Tessa knew that a romance blossomed between Brian and she. In fact, she welcomed it. Unfortunately, she'd promised Katie and her husband that she'd entertain a friend of theirs while he was in town.

This is not something I'd wish on my worst enemy.

Could Tessa get away with killing her best friend? She wondered, as the man who sat across from her and droned on about his coin collections.

He wore a diamond earring, gold chains that dangled in layers around his neck, and a black beard and mustache that looked as if he'd soaked them in baby oil.

Tessa didn't expect another Brian Miller, but good grief, she thought the man she'd been set up with by Katie could at least say one simple sentence that didn't include the word "I." He leered at her as a waiter brought the next course in such a way that led her to believe he expected something in return for supper at such a fine restaurant.

Think again, Buster.

She excused herself to the restroom and snuck out, after paying her half of the bill.

If he acted this way with all his dates she was sure he'd heard every line imaginable to get away from him. Except hers. She left a note with the waiter, which told him she had to get home to her pig.

At home, with the animals secured, she went outside to her front porch to sit and enjoy the warm night.

The moon, full and bright, cast light and shadows around the neighborhood. Sitting on the glider with her feet tucked under her, she rested in the shadows, invisible and observant.

But the shadows didn't hide her from a determined voyeur. Mrs. Henderson had a pair of binoculars pointed right at Tessa.

A thoughtful smile curved her mouth and she saluted the old gossip with her cup of hot chocolate.

Triumph mixed with irritation welled inside her as the woman all but jumped away from the window. Brian would get a kick out of this. She just hoped she didn't have to explain this evening's *other* entertainment to him.

Her elusive peace destroyed, Tessa went inside and, even though it was after nine o'clock, she called Katie.

"I hate you, Katie. You *and* that Tom guy you set me up with. Doesn't your husband know any *nice* guys?"

"You didn't think he was nice? He called and told Paul you'd left him in the lurch. Paul even promised to pay for your meal after Tom's tirade. What on earth happened?"

"Tell Paul I paid for my meal, thank you

very much. And, if he ever tries to find another man for me, I'll have him jailed on conspiracy to commit boredom."

Katie chuckled. "Yeah, I know, I know, your sister is an attorney. I've never met this guy; tell me all about him."

"He's a . . . I don't even know how to describe him." She told her about the ridiculous clothing and jewelry. By the time she got to the collections of priceless pennies and dimes, Katie shrieked with laughter.

"He *does* own a jewelry shop." Her friend said in the man's defense.

"But, he doesn't have to wear the whole store, Katie. You wouldn't believe the lines he used." She mimicked him, " 'I own this and that. I have these coins and these stones. In fact, you look like a ruby to me.' What does that even mean?"

"You can't be serious."

"Oh, yes. Then he said Paul didn't tell him I was so hot."

"Hang on."

In the background Tessa heard Katie's husband's voice. "Ouch! What was that for?"

"For setting my best friend up with Tom, the walking jewelry store." Back to Tessa she said, "I'm sorry. I punished Paul with a smack on the head. Is there anything else you need?"

"Can you ground him this fall from football?"

"I don't have that kind of power. But, I'll make sure the next time he sees Tom he reminds him you paid for your own meal. The jerk would have taken Paul's money."

"I believe *that*."

"Or, *maybe* you just wanted to be with the boy next door?" Katie prompted.

"I won't discuss him. But, let me tell you what I did see." She told her about Mrs. Henderson's binoculars. "I have every intention of confronting that woman."

"Good luck. I'll bet she won't be around again for a while. She'll be watching you and Brian from afar." Tessa heard hesitation in her friend's voice. "Where was your neighbor tonight?"

"I don't know. He didn't call yesterday or today. I think being caught by the snoopy lady put him off."

"I'm sorry, Tess. I know you really like him." Katie then changed the subject to a special meeting at school. After a few moments, Katie hung up.

She's right. Tessa climbed the stairs to start her nightly routine. *No one really competes with Brian. And, I do really like him.*

* * *

Tessa returned fairly early from her "errand." However, Brian noticed, she wasn't dressed for grocery shopping and carried no bags.

He didn't sleep, wondering whether she'd had a date or not. Of course, their budding romance put no ties on the woman, yet, he'd hoped she wouldn't want to see anyone else.

Why? He wasn't going to be around long enough to make this relationship work. What was wrong with him? Did he honestly think he could have a real life?

The next afternoon Brian had a meeting he couldn't miss. No matter what else happened in the world, he had to make this appointment. The day hadn't been one he'd want to repeat. Between an emergency overseas and one in Denver, he thought he'd never get off the phone.

The time he'd planned to use preparing for this meeting was almost gone and he still had things to do. He'd dictate his report on the way downtown and grab a typist from the secretarial pool to take care of it for him.

His exit from his father's house was stopped cold when he saw them. Flowers. Getting out of a van in front of Tessa's house was a deliveryman with a huge bunch of flowers. The size of the bouquet indicated either a proposal or a huge apology, but, either way, serious intent.

He tried to shake off his unease. Some guy sent her flowers. Big deal. He'd taken her flowers. She'd liked them too. Of course, they were from his father and not expensive lilies.

He pulled out from the driveway, failing in his attempt not to watch the delivery in the rear view mirror. The deliveryman turned and headed back to his van and Brian turned back into the drive.

She wasn't home, apparently.

"Problem?" As he approached the van, Brian eyed the bouquet. It had to cost a fortune. Serious intent, indeed.

"Yeah, I need to get these to this address but no one's at home."

Brian checked his watch. She *was* running late. "I can take them."

The guy hesitated, but Brian pulled a twenty out of his pocket and handed it to him. "Here you go. I'll be glad to hold them at my house until Tessa comes home."

Using her first name did the trick and convinced the young man he knew her.

He ran the flowers inside and put them on a table, resisting the temptation to open the card. His father wasn't at home, so he left for his meeting without any other interruptions or questions he didn't want to answer.

At work, however, his mind kept returning to the flowers waiting for Tessa that weren't from him.

His boss called him in the office after the meeting. "Brian, are you feeling alright? You just don't have your usual passion about this deal."

"I'm fine. Just a little tired of living with my father the flower maniac. Get me back out where I belong, Jim. Things will be better."

Jim nodded. "I'll see what I can do. In the meantime, try to not let your father ruin your edge."

As soon as he got in his car, his cell rang. "Brian Miller."

"Who's Paul?" His dad's voice, full of confusion, met his ears.

"Paul who?" Brian returned.

"Someone named Paul sent us flowers and said he was sorry on the card."

Brian's stomach twisted. Sam had read the card on Tessa's flowers. They had to be from a boyfriend with that kind of sentiment.

He hoped he sounded nonchalant. "Oh, those belong to Tessa. She wasn't home when the florist tried to deliver them."

His father sounded relieved. "Okay, I'll take them over, then. Unless you want to?"

"No, Dad." His voice lowered. "You take them." She had what she probably needed and wanted. A man with impeccable taste in flowers who wouldn't be leaving town in a few weeks.

Chapter Six

"**I** should never have let Brian get close to me."

Tessa and Katie sat in the only adult chairs in Tessa's classroom. Tessa lowered her head onto her desk, just missing her lunch plate.

Katie swallowed a bite of her corn dog. "Well, did you really have a choice? I mean the guy just breezed into your life before you knew it, right?"

Tessa wallowed on the papers. "I know, but I still feel, I don't know, tainted, I guess."

Katie grabbed a fry from Tessa's plate. "Someone is a drama queen. I won't mention names; let's just say it's you."

She sat straight up. "I am not! I just don't

like the fact this guy kissed me, knowing he has no real intentions toward me."

"Intentions?" Katie put her food down. "Can you please come back to the future and remember we are in the new millennium?"

"We may be, but I don't want men kissing all over me without even thinking about the consequences."

"Consequences? Do you have a cold or something? A fever blister, maybe?"

Tessa huffed. "I want a long-term relationship. Is that too much to ask, even in the new millennium?" She lowered her head again.

Katie's stern voice met her ears. "How do you know what Brian's thinking? Have you asked him? And, sit up. I'll put you in time-out if you don't."

Disconcerted, Tessa raised her head but pointedly looked at her plate. "It was nice of your husband to apologize, but Paul's flowers ended up at Brian's house and his father brought them to me."

Katie's eyes grew wide. "Really? Did he say anything?"

"He said he's glad I'd found a way to keep the pig at home, and he hoped he hadn't hurt my feelings about it."

"No Brian news, then?"

"No. But, Brian's car was in the drive later, so he saw them."

Katie looked thoughtful a moment. "I wonder . . ." she broke off with a giggle.

"What?"

"Do you think he believes Paul is your boyfriend?"

A wry grin played at Tessa's lips. "I wondered that too."

With a drink of her cola, Katie put down the can. "The plot thickens."

Later at home, she opened the front door to the porch and found Paul before her with more flowers, wine, and candy. She laughed at the sight of him so laden down and couldn't help but throw her arms around him right there. "You're forgiven, Paul. You've been forgiven for, well, to be honest, about a split second now."

"Aren't we a scene for your nosy neighbor?"

"I hope so! While she talks about me, she's giving someone else a break."

Tessa pulled away. "You didn't have to bring anything."

"I know. But, Katie will be here any moment and I'm trying to impress her with my thoughtfulness."

She pulled him inside as she spoke. "Uh, huh. What did you do this time?"

He put his goodies on the coffee table and flopped down on the couch. "Simply said: Anniversary. Last week. Forgot. Dog house."

"Ah. Now you bring all the good stuff and hope she'll forgive you, right?"

"I also bought her a present that she will show off tomorrow at school with the word *forgiveness* written all over it."

"Yeah." She motioned for him to follow her into the kitchen. "That means jewelry. Did you buy it from Tom, the walking jewelry store?"

"Yes. At a discount. Oh, man, don't tell Katie that or I'm back to step one."

Katie arrived in short order and dinner progressed as planned.

Paul made a sincere apology and Katie responded in kind. She leaned forward and gave him a buzz on the cheek and Paul wrapped his wife in a hug.

Tessa studied her friends' affection with envy.

Paul and Katie were constantly at play. No hard feelings really existed.

Tessa, lost in her own thoughts, heard Katie speak to her.

"You with us?" She touched Tessa's hand.

"Yes, Ma'am, I'm with you. A toast!" Tessa lifted her glass of tea in a salute.

"To what shall we toast?" Paul raised his glass to join the women.

Katie answered, "To Tessa. May you find a man who will be at your side."

"And, to you guys," Tessa returned, "many happy anniversaries." She put aside her loneliness and concentrated on having a nice time with her friends.

The glasses clinked.

Later, Katie left early to pick up their children at the sitter's, while Paul helped Tessa clean up.

When most of it was complete, he left, but not without a big hug on the front porch, mostly for Mrs. Henderson's binoculars.

But, other eyes caught the scene as well.

Brian saw her as he approached his father's house. Her blond hair blew behind her in the breeze, loose around her shoulders. He'd gone to the store but before he left, he'd seen her.

He didn't expect to see her. Not on the porch in the arms of another man. He thought she had feelings for him and . . . what else?

Why was he so shocked? He'd seen the flowers. He knew what the card said.

Purposefully, he'd stayed gone a while to

divert himself from thinking about her. He hoped the man would be gone when he returned, but the red car, still parked on the street, pulled into traffic before Brian turned into the drive.

Tessa stood on the porch, waving at the occupant.

What did he expect? That she should wait on him to decide to quit a job he loved just so she could have a nice settled life?

He stopped the car, turned the key, and slammed the door shut with more force than necessary.

Before he could get into the house, Tessa called to him. He looked around to see her get first Lilly's then Joey's leashes. "Brian?"

He approached and stood on the other side of the fence. "You really like living here, don't you?"

She stared, complete surprise on her face. "Of course. Is that a problem?"

"You love to teach and come home and plant flowers and work around the house, don't you?" He gestured to his father's flowerbeds as an example, an edge to his voice.

"Guilty as charged. What's this all about?"

"Absolutely nothing. Have a nice night." He

pivoted on his heel and entered his father's house through the back door, into the kitchen. He dropped his shopping bag on the table.

Sam had left a note that said he'd be back soon, so Brian began the task of putting away the groceries. He stifled a groan when his pager sounded. As he picked up the phone to dial the number, he wondered how much longer he'd be in town to handle these problems; he always had an emergency . . . somewhere. He picked up the phone and called his office. Moments later he found himself on the way there. Just another reason no real relationship would work.

A few days later, Brian pulled his SUV into a slot at a local sandwich shop. He could order to go and get back to the office, though he admitted, he'd rather not go back to that mad house.

"Hey, Paul! Good to see you!" The guy behind the deli counter greeted the man in line in front of Brian. Unimpressed they knew each other, he stepped a little closer to the counter. In his peripheral vision, he recognized the man the waiter had called Paul.

Tessa's boyfriend. Here. At my favorite deli. Of course, that's nothing to me, it's not like Tessa and I had more than a date or two. The guy looked at Brian and smiled. "How's it going?"

"Fine, and you?" Brian nodded and tried to hide a small stab of jealousy.

"Doing good. Hey, Lenny, I'll have a meatball sub on wheat and a . . ." Paul's voice trailed as he studied the menu behind the counter.

"We just pulled some rye out of the oven, Paul."

"Oh, that sounds great, give me a ham and cheese on that, will you?"

"Sure thing." The man turned to Brian, "And, you sir?"

"I'll have the ham and cheese on rye too. With an extra pickle. To go."

He tried to stop himself, to no avail. "You know Tessa Price, don't you?"

"Huh? Oh, yeah, Tess. Everyone loves Tessa. She's a great gal."

Everyone?

"You know her?" Paul countered.

"I live in her area." Not completely a lie. Not completely the truth either, but that was beside the point.

"You don't live next door where the guy has that garden, do you?"

"That's my dad's flowers."

"I wish I could get my place to look that good."

The waiter brought Paul his food. "Thanks." Then, to Brian he said, "Nice talking to you."

A curt nod was Brian's good-bye. He quickly paid for his food and headed for the door. *Everyone loves Tessa.* His mind repeated the words.

The jealousy thing, it would go away. He knew it would.

Brian got in his car. Not good. Not good to feel like this. Not good to want a real life. Not good at all.

His cell phone sounded, interrupting his lunch and preoccupation with Tessa.

A few days of Brian waving from the driveway made Tessa long to be near him. She always received a smile. Always a nice word about the weather, the flowers, the pig. But, he wasn't coming over. He didn't ask her out.

She missed him.

When the phone rang, Tessa hoped. But it was only Danni calling her with a reminder of Joey's day at the county fair. Danni had entered him in the pet show and Tessa would have to take him to be groomed.

Tessa dreaded it like the plague.

If he didn't show any more respect to the groomer than to Tessa she might have to pay extra. She worried the person grooming him might not ever do it again.

How does one groom a pig, anyway?

She clipped his leash on and led him through the back door, Lilly behind them, whining to follow. "Not this time, Lilly," Tessa gently warned, "I'll be right back to take you for a walk."

When she got out the door, Brian stood at his car dressed for the office, getting his brief case and other things from the vehicle.

"Brian?"

He turned to face her and looked taken aback. "No school?"

"I took a personal day." She gestured towards Joey. "He has to have some things done today. Special grooming for the fair."

Could the situation be anymore uncomfortable?

He nodded. "Have a good time."

Before she thought her mouth opened and the words came pouring out. "Which is, of course, a joke in itself." She walked toward her own car with the agony of defeat.

"Hey, Tess? Do you need any help with him?"

Twisting around to look at him, she offered

him a small, shy smile. "Always. But, I'm just supposed to drop him off. I could fix you dinner when I get back, though."

"Appreciate it, but I've got work." He pointed to his briefcase to prove his point.

"See you later!" She put Joey in the car and tried to keep her disappointment at bay.

When she reached their destination, she finally hit a run of good luck. The pet groomer Danni used for Joey had an emergency and ran so far behind she asked if she could keep him overnight and groom him first thing in the morning. No charge for the kenneling.

Tessa, though she acted discontented, agreed. Readily.

She returned to find Brian dressed in jeans, leaning against his car. "So, what's for dinner?"

"I thought it was work."

"Just didn't find that as appealing as a good home cooked meal."

She didn't try to curb her enthusiasm. "I think we'll have barbequed chicken and roasted potatoes."

He strolled over to her and opened the back door, greeting Lilly along the way. "I like the sound of that."

They amicably cooked together, Brian fitting into her kitchen, her house, and her world as if he belonged there. When she shared her "distress" of a night without the world's favorite pig, Brian burst into good-natured laughter.

Dinner started well, both of them feeding Lilly from the table, which was an absolute no-no for the dog. But, somewhere along the line Brian sensed tension. He thought he might as well begin the talk they needed to have. "I saw your flowers in the front room. They're nice."

"Yeah. A friend making up for a mistake."

He nodded, but hesitated to speak. "So, you didn't make up with a boyfriend, or anything?"

"No, just a friend who owed me an apology. He's married to the lady I teach with. They were here last night."

Why did relief wash over him when he knew what he had to do? "I didn't see a woman."

"She may have left before you got here, she had to go by the sitter's." She wiped her mouth with her napkin.

Apology tinged his voice. "Tessa, I thought you should know, my dad heard rumors about us in the neighborhood, and Mrs. Weathers made a comment to me as well."

"I'm not surprised, nor am I concerned." She ran a finger along the rim of her water glass.

"Good ole Mrs. H. got down and dirty about what she saw. She added a lot to it. You didn't come out looking very good."

"I'm sure it won't be the last time." Her gaze did not lift from her glass. "Brian, why are you living with your dad? I don't mean to be nosy, but Mrs. Henderson tells an exciting story, that as you say, leaves you not looking good."

"My apartment was destroyed by the neighbors. I just heard today that my landlord is ready to settle. Whatever you were told, I'm sure is more interesting than the truth."

"I heard you punched out the neighbor."

His laugh was contagious. "If you'd seen the guy, you'd be glad I'm smart enough to run from him."

Just a few moments ago they were able to fill the room with small talk, but now a heavy silence fell on them.

They'd finished their meal when he sipped from his water glass. "I'll be going back on the road in a couple of weeks."

She got up and put her plate in the sink. "That's your job. No reason to hang around when there's money to be made, right?"

"Something like that, yeah." The warm atmosphere cooled to a chill.

"Then, I suggest you go to wherever it is you go and consult until the cows come home."

"Or the pigs?"

He saw her smile as plastic. "You've got it."

"I'm glad you understand. I thought maybe I'd led you to think otherwise—"

"Don't worry, Brian. It takes more than a few hugs and kisses to make a relationship. Didn't mean a thing to me." She dismissed it all with a wave of her hand.

"I didn't mean to offend you. Or to put you in a position where I leave you here to deal with the gossip."

"I've taken worse. Believe me. I'm the youngest of three, remember?"

"As a matter of fact, I do remember." He stood. "I really need to leave. I've got a break-fast meeting in the morning." He followed her to the back door. "You know, my sister Emily is coming up on Sunday and you're more than welcome to meet her."

She stood aloof. "That is sweet, Brian, but I'm busy. Sorry."

"That's okay, another time, maybe."

"Sure."

He walked back to his father's, going straight to his room. After he brushed his teeth and got ready for bed, he wondered if he did the right thing. Telling her he planned to leave could only be good, right?

It was, in fact, the fair thing to do. He didn't want her to think there could be a future with him. Not with all the traveling he did.

He situated himself in bed, his arms folded and hands stacked behind his head. If that was so right, why did he feel so terrible?

Out of pure and total desperation to be busy as she'd told Brian she would be, she'd invited Paul and Katie to Sunday dinner and what did they do? They brought along another one of Paul's friends. Not twenty minutes into the evening, and Tessa wanted to kill someone.

Why had she told Katie about her conversation with Brian? Now, every man they knew that was single, regardless of age, prison record, or body odor, would be knocking on her door.

And, Katie would blame Paul, but *he* didn't do this to her. No, he may know the men, but Katie was the one with the plan.

Tessa sighed. She didn't want to hurt anyone's feelings, but she just couldn't bring herself to date these men. Like Ken. Not that the guy looked like Frankenstein. He looked pretty good, in a blond, not as tall as Brian, not as lean as Brian, sort of way.

He just didn't like anything all evening.

Nothing.

He hated the fresh broccoli soup she made. "Broccoli gets between my teeth, you know."

The salad had too much dressing. "Whew! This must be an advertisement for vinegar."

The entrée, a serving of shrimp scampi and a loaded baked potato didn't please him either. "Don't care much for seafood. The potato isn't really done well enough, but I can eat it."

Tessa had had enough. "You know Ken, I do have peanut butter and jelly. The jelly is home-made, in fact."

"That's real nice of you, Tessa, but I can get this down. It's not like it's spoiled or anything." He acted as if he were giving her a compliment.

She wanted to choke, or better yet, choke him. "I'm so glad."

Before she could say anything else, Katie jumped up from her chair. "Tessa, why don't you and I go into the kitchen and check on dessert?"

She could barely conceal her frustration. "I didn't make any dessert, Katie dear."

"We brought a devil's food cake. We really should cut it."

"That's great. I'll get the knife." She turned her eyes to Ken. "Won't you excuse us?"

"Sure, Tessa, but no cake for me, I'm allergic to chocolate." He winked at her.

She only nodded as she left. *It figures. Allergic to my favorite food group.*

In the kitchen, Katie warned her, "Don't even think I'm letting you near a knife, little girl."

Tessa leaned against the countertop. "I'm past being offended and now I just want to laugh. Are all men like that? I think he'd find a reason to complain about paradise."

Tessa met Katie's eyes and started chuckling again. Her friend joined in and soon they were hugging each other, faces wet with tears.

"Why on earth did you guys bring him with you?"

"Paul is convinced you need a husband. It's honestly not me."

"But, he had to get that impression from someone. Who could it be? Let me think." Tessa glared.

Katie grabbed a butter knife from the kitchen drawer. "I wouldn't know. It's not like I told him you needed one. Or, to fix you up with men he knew."

A knock on the backdoor kept Katie safe.

Tessa opened it to find Brian on her step, Joey in hand.

"You have my pig." She could certainly make a flirtatious statement when the need arose.

"He's back in business. Somehow, he got Lilly to chew on the rope and I found him in Dad's flowers. She's still chewing on some of it."

Tessa heard Katie clear her throat. "I'm sorry, Brian. Come in a minute and meet my friends Katie and Paul."

"I really can't Tessa, but thanks." He waved at Katie. "Maybe next time. I was leaving when I found the Wonder Pig in Dad's tulips."

He stepped off the porch but turned back to her. "Are you going to be at the block party?"

"A week from yesterday. I'd planned to, why?"

"I wanted to know because from what my dad has heard, we're in for some of Mrs. Henderson's jibes."

Tessa boiled. That comment just topped her day. "I'll be there now, or die."

"I'll see you then." He stepped off the porch and out of sight.

When Tessa turned around to find Katie standing holding the knife, her mouth open. "You okay?"

"*That* is the boy next door?"

"The one and only." Tessa tucked Joey under her arm and closed the door.

"Gosh, Tessa, no wonder you're pining for him. He's drop dead gorgeous."

"I'm not pining." Joey snorted a complaint at being held so tightly and she deposited him on the floor. He scuffled off in a hurry, probably to plan another escape.

Tessa washed her hands and then eyed the chocolate cake greedily. One taste wouldn't hurt. She scooped a little frosting from its side and licked her finger clean of chocolate. "I just wish things could be different. That's all. There's other fish in the sea."

"There's a nice flounder in the dining room with Paul right now."

They placed three pieces of cake on plates and Tessa put some vanilla ice cream in a bowl in the hopes Ken could eat it.

"No wonder Ken and Tom don't compare," Katie mumbled.

No wonder.

Tessa's preoccupation with Brian made the company of others uncomfortable for everyone. After only another thirty minutes or so, they left.

Ken promised to call her.

Tessa hoped he didn't.

Later, she couldn't sleep. After a long, hot

bath, Tess heard Brian return home. The sister had been there today as well. She'd heard them all laughing and saw the barbeque grill still smoldering this evening.

They left before Brian returned from his . . . errand? Date, maybe? Who knew? She cringed. A nice restaurant and ride with the moon roof of his SUV open.

What a plan. But, she had other things to tend to. Her home, her students. She heard something scratch at the door.

And, for now, a pig.

He had to stay in the house, even if she had to try to get him to use kitty litter. He just couldn't be trusted outside.

But, he had to go.

When she returned him to the house, she decided to stay out for a moment or two. Though it was almost midnight Tessa sat down on the porch in the darkness. The last few weeks twirled in her mind.

Had it been four months since she'd moved into the new house? She added it on her fingers.

It had.

Danni and Mike had left over two weeks ago. Just one more week of the "visitors."

According to their conversation, Brian would leave in a couple of weeks. From what she could tell, he stayed away for months at a time. Or at least weeks. And she would be alone. She pulled her terry robe tight against the chill and sipped her warm tea. After sunset the temperatures dropped dramatically in Tennessee this time of year. A cold wave, per the weather report, would set in tonight and last most of the week.

She remembered the block party this weekend. Being a spectacle, the subject of Mrs. Henderson's stories, would be difficult to bear.

The woman's idle gossip angered her, but she knew no fear of her. She braced herself emotionally for the battle. With her mood being what it was, Mrs. Henderson may want to rethink her ramblings and finger pointing.

"Of course, I could always not go." If she didn't, she'd let Brian know. He showed himself gracious enough to warn her, it was the least she could do.

She had other options. Tennis with Katie, for an example. They were equally matched and usually had fun when they played. They could go to the park, and afterwards check out a movie or go to the mall.

Unless of course, Paul decided to "help" her with another male friend.

She knew they just wanted her to be happy. They didn't want to see her by herself.

Still, here she sat without even the pig to keep her company. And, even if they went out and had a good time, at the end of the day she would be alone.

By then Danni would be back and they could shop or sit at their house and play chess. Michael always beat her. She demanded a new game quite often.

Sighing, Tessa stood and went inside, closed up the house, and went to bed. Instead of finding escape in sleep, however, she tossed and turned, ending up on her back.

Pretty soon when she got home in the evening there would be no animals. Or anyone else. So, once again, she would be alone.

She sat straight up in the bed. At this moment Tom and Ken didn't look so bad. Well, Tom did, but maybe if she let Ken do the cooking, she could stomach him.

I'm pathetic. She plopped back down; exhaustion finally overtook her and she dropped off into a restless sleep.

Brian couldn't find anything right with his world.

This coffee could walk over to the cashier by itself. The breakfast meeting went well, with the exception of the food. The client's choice of restaurant had left much to be desired, though it was known for its early morning cuisine. He knew the food to be good, as he'd eaten there before, but knowing this meeting would send him on the road—and away from Tessa—just made the fare sawdust in his mouth.

He took another drink of the bitter mixture and tried to smile for his audience of one. Nothing seemed the same now that he'd met Tessa.

"Your ideas, Brian, are remarkable. I hadn't thought of any of the things you've brought to the table today. I'm sure we can use your services, but on one condition."

He kept his voice indulgent. "I'll do my best to accommodate you."

"My company will sign the contract today, if *you* will do the actual hands-on work."

Denver, Colorado. "It would be my pleasure." For the first time since he took this job, he didn't want to go wherever the job led.

He wanted to be home. But he really didn't have a home, did he?

The men finished their meal with the usual small talk.

Brian's thoughts weren't where they needed to be. He should be excited; he'd just pulled in another big client. But instead, the subject of his thoughts lived next door.

He didn't want to live in a hotel room, even with the luxuries of room service, indoor pools and spas, and maid service. He wanted to cook and laugh and even help clean up, with a little pig oinking at his feet.

He wanted to be with Tessa.

"How soon do you think you'll want me in Denver?" Brian asked the words before he knew they were out of his mouth.

"We'll start you in the Fort White office. So, next Monday will be fine. As for Denver, they'll be some things to work out before I have an answer for you on that." Mr. Tolliver smiled at him. "Probably within the next three weeks."

Brian turned the charm up a notch. "The mile-high city in the summer. I think I'll like this job."

Chapter Seven

"I have to give you credit, Miss Price. That is one of the smartest animals I've ever seen." Mr. Miller was very kind with his statement, considering Joey had just rooted up two of his tulips. "I know he actually got the dog to chew the rope at one point. He's rooted up the peg you've tied him to. But, I don't know how he did it this time."

Tessa stood in the backyard, studying the chain that should have held Joey fastened to the tree. "I don't get it. I had him chained."

Mr. Miller's face echoed her confusion. "I'll be honest with you, I'm so baffled about this, I don't have the heart to be angry."

Brian's arrival pulled them away from their bewilderment.

He got out of the car and joined them.

Tessa's stomach rolled with . . . dread? Anticipation? Whatever it was, she felt a little queasy.

"What did he do now?" His nonchalance irked her, even though she knew it shouldn't.

"He's been at it again," Sam told him, his voice still laced with confusion.

Brian stooped and picked up the steel chain and scrutinized it. After a moment or two he looked from side to side. Five minutes of silence from all and Brian stood up and brushed his hands off. "You've got me. This time, I'm going to say the little guy is a genius and leave it at that."

She found it hard to remain coherent so close to Brian. She hoped her voice didn't give away her emotions. "I guess I'll just tie him back up and watch to see what he does."

"I know what he'll do." The older man's smile became infectious. "He'll use a welding torch to get out of it." With that, he left Tess and Brian alone. The tension could be cut with a knife.

"Is Houdini in the house?" Brian finally asked.

She should go in, but she didn't. "Yeah. I thought it the safest place for him."

"Well, have a good evening."

"You too." She sounded polite and without a care in the world. Exactly the way she wanted to sound.

Brian took a few steps and turned around. "Look, I have a dinner I should attend tonight."

"I'd better let you go then."

"I wondered—and I know it's short notice because I hadn't planned to go at all—but would you like to go?"

"Why?"

"There are several reasons."

"Such as?"

"We'll have a good time."

"We might. I have things to do, though."

"I know, but I'm sure there are a hundred other reasons you should go with me. I just can't think of all of them right now."

She fought a battle of personal restraint, but lost. "Why not?"

This wasn't Tessa's first time at The Depot, but never had it looked so regal. Instead of the usual comfortable railroad motif, she found surprising elegance. The linens, a royal purple, complimented the silver, polished until it shined.

Known for hosting premier events, the party confirmed The Depot's excellent reputation. A live band played from the stage. No karaoke jockey here. These people, whoever they were, meant business.

A man named Gerard Owen and his wife, April, greeted Brian and Tessa as they arrived. The gentleman, older than they, introduced them to other guests and worked the room as many entertainers wooed a crowd.

Dancing, food, wine, and great conversation—the Owens' had thought of everything. Tessa enjoyed herself, even as she assumed the role of Brian's girlfriend. She had to admit, however, he played the part in return. Attentive, sweet, and even a little guarded when a gentleman made a play for her, Brian was the perfect date.

Laughing at one of his colleague's jokes, Tessa looked over to see Brian with another woman. They appeared to be deep in conversation. Knowing her time with Brian was short, Tessa wandered over to where they stood.

Brian didn't look as if he were at all concerned about her joining them. He introduced her to the owner of the company he worked for, Sherry Beacher, an elegant lady to say the least. With Brian's hand possessively at the small of Tessa's back, the three stood together talking, laughing, and enjoying the finger foods that occasionally floated by on silver platters.

Sherry explained to Tessa the ins and outs of sending Brian out of town to the initial consultation, making the business plans that the other employees would then put into work for each client.

"We can't live without him." Sherry took a sip of her drink. "But, I suppose you feel the same way."

Sherry watched the couple with an all-seeing eye. Tessa knew this woman didn't miss a trick. Or the look Tessa and Brian shared at her comment.

Before Brian could comment, Jim Powell joined them. "So, this is the girl that has your mind on other things than work. He needs to watch that, huh, Sherry?"

"I think the man's allowed a personal life. As much as he's done for us. If you'll excuse me, I think that's Peyton. I want to go over and say hello."

Jim reeked of tension. "When do you leave for Denver?"

Brian answered Jim with hesitation. "It'll

be a few weeks, yet. By the way, did you see the figures on Kewell Toys?"

"Of course I have." The man's voice, full of defense, boomed louder than needed. "They look fine to me. Is there a problem?"

Brian studied his boss. "No problem. Just wondering if you'd seen them."

Fate, the four-letter word that it is, changed the party at that moment. Brian became different, slightly withdrawn, and definitely distant.

They were the first to leave. An odd tension hung in the air on the ride home. Brian tried to make small talk and even smile, but the distance that had come between them at the party lingered.

When they pulled into the drive, he apologized. "I'm sorry we left so early, I need to do some work I forgot about."

"No, you don't."

"Excuse—"

"Jim became defensive, so you're going to look over the figures that you discussed. Am I right?"

He took a long breath and sighed. "Yeah. You are."

"I would do the same thing. I could tell you were thrown off kilter by his actions. I don't know the man, but I realized he got uncomfortable when you asked about Kewell Toys."

He smiled and Tessa knew at that moment she was head over heels for this guy.

"Just think, Brian, you weren't even going to go to the party."

"Only because I didn't have a date. Then, I ended up with the most beautiful woman there."

"Oh, go on." She told him. "I mean it, keep going."

He laughed aloud. "I never know what to expect from you."

"It keeps you on your toes, right?"

"Yeah. It does. It also makes me want to do this." With a hand slipped behind her head, he kissed her. She loved the feel of his lips on hers. He could do this forever, and she'd be happy.

After a few moments, and feeling dizzy from his affection, Tessa pulled away. "The block party is just a few days off; let's not give the neighborhood any more fat to chew on."

Brian shifted uncomfortably. "I never dreamed I'd come home and meet you and feel like this, Tessa." He became quiet for a moment, not looking at her. "I'm gone about nine months out of the year. I'll be leaving in a week or two and be gone for at least three months, possibly four. Can you live like that?"

She didn't have to be hit over the head. She

knew exactly what he wanted her to say. It broke her heart not to oblige him. "No, Brian. I can't."

He turned back and faced her. "Would you consider going with me?"

"Give up my career and follow you all over the globe?" She shook her head. "Fun and exciting, for about six months. Then I'd need stability. A place to call home. Somewhere to raise children."

"I know."

"If you knew, why'd you ask?"

"I had to hear you say it."

Tessa sighed and opened her door. Brian tried to make it around the car to help her, but the gallant gesture was lost to the conversation.

"We can't make this work, Brian."

He didn't speak, only nodded.

"Thanks for taking me. Good night."

She went inside, not waiting for his answer.

Upon her entrance to the living room, Lilly turned over and wagged her tail, and Joey snorted, but both animals resumed their tangled position and returned to snoring.

Loneliness crept into her bones like she'd never known.

It didn't leave her while she slept, tossing and turning. The next day, as she tried to concentrate on her usual daily activities, she still ached with it.

She refused to be overwhelmed by emotion. Her nature didn't allow that.

That afternoon she let Joey and Lilly out into the yard. Lilly she tied to the stake. But Joey she tied around a small tree, this time with two chains.

"I'm too smart for my own good." She watched as the pig tried to get away and couldn't. With a sigh of relief, Tessa made sure each animal had its own food and water and went inside with a deep sigh of satisfaction. "I may even take a nap today." *What is it the Australians say? Oh, yeah, no worries.* She changed from a summer dress into a pair of cutoffs and a tee shirt. This change in the atmosphere of her home fit her well.

No worries.

"I am a lucky woman." She flopped onto the couch. "I have no worries. Pets and a new house, what more could a working woman want? And, the pets are only on loan, so *they* can't even worry me." Her thoughts wandered to Brian. "No man to make problems in my life."

After picking up her TV remote, she flipped it on and channel surfed. "No worries." She knew if she repeated it enough she might begin to believe her own words.

A sigh escaped her lips. "I said no worries and I meant it."

"You're off your game, Brian." His boss didn't like the ideas he had for a new client.

"Excuse me? Off my game?"

"You heard me." Jim Powell took a drink of his coffee and leaned back in his chair, his eyebrows raised. "So, is it what's her name from last night?"

"Tessa Price?" Brian looked at Jim, then behind him for the waitress. He wanted some ketchup for his french fries before they got cold.

"When a guy like you quits hitting the mark, it's always a woman."

"I just failed the pop quiz, so now I'm a has-been?" He motioned the waitress to the table. She brought ketchup with her.

"Thanks." Brian smiled at her then turned a frown to Jim. "I don't appreciate you giving up on me so easily. You owe me, big guy."

"Because you've been worth your weight in gold? Because you took the company from this little tiny new guy on the block and made it one of the big guys in the business?"

"Something like that, yeah."

"I'm grateful. But, you've got to give it your best if you want to stay in the game. Remember, love means nothing."

"I think that's Tennis."

"*I* think you're going to be finding a job at home in a few months from the way you've been walking around the office lately. Like I told you, the Fort White office doesn't need you. You'll be going out of town if you want to stay with us."

Brian thought about what Jim said for a long moment, and then slouched back in his chair, disgusted. "I'm so glad we've had this little talk. First, about how I made the company for you, then how I may need to look for another job. I appreciate your words of loyalty and wisdom, Jim. Really. It's too much."

"Just want you to know, I won't hold you up. You want out, you get out, but the job is number one."

Brian wiped his mouth with his napkin, stood, and reached in his pocket. He took enough out to cover his part of the meal and a tip. "That will come out of my expense account." With that, he walked to the cashier, got his ticket, and left.

Not one to use foul language, Brian surprised even himself when he got in the car and cursed Jim to high heavens. Anger ebbed and flowed in him like a tide.

Jim told him he'd made Enhancement Consultants, now get out. Not only that, Brian had looked over the Kewell Toys figures again. They needed work. Or, maybe they'd already been worked on. Brian wasn't sure.

He did know one thing, though. Evidently, Jim wanted him gone. Either on the road, or out altogether.

He pulled into the parking garage of the firm. Maybe Jim wasn't far off base on all the things he said. "You know what, Jim? We're about to find out what you're made of."

Chapter Eight

Tonight was *the* night. Tessa worried about this evening since Danni left on vacation. But, now it was here. Joey, neatly groomed, sported a big, blue collar and snorted proudly as the two of them made their way to the car.

Brian pulled in just as she got him in the car.

"Is everything alright?"

"No, my stomach is churning. Tonight is pet night at the county fair and guess who's going."

With his briefcase in hand, he stopped and looked at her as if she had two heads. "Joey is entered?"

She gave a forced smile and tense nod. "He came in second last year."

"No kidding?"

"Nope. Right behind a French poodle that made a doodle when she was announced."

He burst into laughter. "I'd have paid to see that."

"Five dollars and you can go this year."

She saw a gleam of interest in his eyes, before he looked at his briefcase.

"Unless you have to work, of course."

The smile that met her gaze, white against his tanned skin, nearly left her breathless. *Katie is right. You have it bad.*

"You know what, Miss Price? I'd love to come see you and my favorite pig in the pet show. Let me run inside. Just five minutes, okay?"

"Sure." She didn't care if it was just on a friendship basis. She wanted to be near him and this was just as good a time as any. Soon he'd leave and it would be much easier to accept the inevitable. For now, she could at least enjoy herself in his company.

A few moments later, Brian emerged from the back door. He'd changed from his business suit to a pair of jeans and nice pullover shirt. He looked incredible to be dressed so casual.

She pulled herself together and said, "Get in."

He obeyed with a smile.

On the way to the fair grounds, they talked amicably. Tessa could sense something different about him. The tension of the other night now gone, as if suddenly he had no problems. She had no idea what it was, but she liked it.

They got to the fairgrounds and found a parking spot. She got Joey out and the little devil was a gentleman pig.

Brian voiced his amazement. "Shouldn't he be giving you a hard time right about now?"

"It's the collar."

"What do you mean?"

They walked towards the pavilion where Joey would compete. "Joey has on his show collar. When it's on him, he's great."

"Why don't you leave it on him?"

"Because then it wouldn't be special and he'd act like he always does, even during a show."

After their arrival at the pet show arena, Tessa registered Joey and led her group to its seats. Joey, perched in front of them, curiously glanced around.

Other animals were marched around, asked to do tricks—all the things Brian expected. Some were beautiful animals. Some did not want to be there and had to be pulled and prodded. Others appeared sweet and demure.

He especially liked a big, blue-eyed husky

called Smoky. He felt guilty rooting for the other animal.

But soon it was Joey's turn.

Afraid he'd have to give Tessa oxygen, Brian watched her with her nephew.

Oinking noises came from the audience of about two hundred people. The unkindness didn't set well with Brian.

Joey, however, made them stand up and take notice when the pig obeyed all commands and Tessa led him into several tricks that Brian didn't know he could do. They took another stroll in front of the judges. Brian's breath caught for Tessa when Joey stopped with her and actually bowed to them.

The audience went wild, a change of heart Brian didn't expect.

"He has a shot at this," he marveled to himself.

Tessa brought Joey back and sat down. Brian couldn't help but pat her back and try to comfort her.

"How'd we do?"

"I think the judges loved the finale. I know everyone else did."

Tessa rung her hands but didn't answer.

"You don't need to be so nervous. He did great, and so did you."

"Thanks."

Brian found the whole ridiculous thing appealing. He looked at Tessa; happy he'd made the decision to come with her.

When the winners were announced Brian took Tessa's hand, liking the way it fit snugly inside his.

One of the judges, an older man with graying hair, and a teen to hold the ribbons for him, strode to the center of the arena.

"I've been asked by my fellow judges to announce the winners. First, we would like to thank our sponsors, Sybil's Dog Food, for their support of our yearly event. The proceeds, as I'm sure you're aware, go directly to the animal shelter." The judge had a microphone that everyone in the large arena could hear. "And, now, our placements. Third place, goes to: Smoky the Husky, owned by Benjamin Davis." The winning couple joined him in the center spot. "Young man, your dog is not only a gorgeous animal, he's well behaved and there is a sweetness in his personality that we could all feel."

Brian and Tessa applauded. Brian understood what the man said. There *was* something special about the dog.

"Second place: Joey Sommers and his Aunt Tessa Price." Brian hugged Tessa in excitement before she and Joey trotted to the center.

He certainly hoped Tessa wasn't disappointed with second place again.

"The pig's bow deserved something. We couldn't believe he bowed for us. Next you'll teach him to courtesy."

The audience howled with laughter.

"And, now, first place: P.C. the cat and owner Bonnie Dawson. A cat that could be taught *anything*, with their usual reserved personalities, should be held in high esteem. We admit it, though, it was the handshake that clenched the blue ribbon."

On the way home, Tessa called her sister. Brian drove her car while they talked. Danni was obviously thrilled with second place and excited that she and Mike would be home over the weekend to get their "children."

Brian checked the clock on the dash. He couldn't believe it was after ten; no wonder he was so tired. They pulled into the drive.

"Do you mind if I come in a minute? I'd like to talk to you."

Tessa didn't understand, but she didn't refuse.

She got Joey settled then she sat down on the couch. "Shoot."

"I have something I have to say."

A flicker of apprehension coursed through her. "Okay."

"I think . . . I may be in love with you."

She gasped without thinking about it. "I—"

"If things were different with my job, do you think we could make things work?"

She tried not to let her emotions carry her away. "I'd like that."

"Then give me a couple of weeks. Can you do that?" His eyes shone with purpose.

She could barely lift her voice above a whisper. "I'll wait."

When Tessa got home from work the next day, a huge bouquet of cut flowers greeted her on the back porch. The note read, "I'm bringing supper around seven. B."

It wasn't until seven fifteen that he made his appearance. It looked as if he'd had better days.

"Are you okay?" She helped him put Chinese takeout boxes on the bar. "You look as if you've been through the ringer."

"I have. The job is rough right now." He kissed her quickly on the forehead. "But I don't want to talk about that. It's one of those things I'd rather leave at the office."

"At least you have an excuse for running late." She quipped.

"I said *around* seven. Not at seven."

"You can't be tardy when you date a teacher."

Humor danced in his eyes. "Can you remind me of that one more time? That you're a teacher, I mean. See, I keep forgetting. If it will make you feel better, then by all means write it in your diary—or is it your grade book? I'm late tonight. Don't forget the part about the horrible day though." He grabbed two plates from the cupboard and laid out rice and vegetables on them.

Their conversation flowed easily. By the time the evening drew to a close, they'd made their way to the front steps.

"I don't know about these seats on the steps, Tessa. After all, the block's spies are everywhere."

"Just one spy. I hope she sees everything. She's talked about you and my pig enough."

"I'm sure whatever she said about me is an exaggeration. Or a complete lie. Take your pick." He changed the subject. "Aren't you going to tie Joey up to that chair?"

"Not in the mood for a run. I put the ribbon where he can see it. He knows it means something special."

"That's a smart pig. Don't you think?"

"As long as we don't have to chase the little guy, he can be as special as he wants to be."

Brian yawned. "The party's over, Hon. I've got to get up early in the morning."

"It's only," she looked at her watch, "five minutes after one."

An embrace and sweet kiss ended the evening.

She went to bed without the usual loneliness. She slept sounder and woke up happier than she had in quite a while.

The next day in school, she didn't tell Katie. Paul still thought his life's calling was to find her a husband. She felt almost guilty about the way things were working out with Brian.

She wished she had said something on Thursday when Brian and she had just gotten home from some shopping and a knock came on the door. Paul and another man of the hour stood on her front porch.

She wished she could think of a time when she was more embarrassed. But, at this point, she couldn't.

His friend eyed her appreciatively.

Paul smiled like a Cheshire cat. "Hi, Tess. I'd like you to meet my buddy, Tony. We wanted to ask you to go to the park and cheer us on in a sandlot game."

Both of the men wore jeans and tee shirts.

Tony winked at her. "We could certainly use some cheering. We've lost the last two games. A sweet lady, such as yourself, would do wonders for our morale."

The words are nice, but the leer gives me the willies. "Another time, perhaps," she addressed Paul, "Brian and I just got here and I'm too tired to do much cheering."

They said their good-byes, but, as they left, Tessa could hear Tony. "You said she was desperate; who's Brian?"

After the door closed, Tessa locked it. She didn't want anymore door-to-door blind dates interfering with her evening.

A lawyer show on TV had Brian's full attention when she entered the room. She sat down close to him on the couch and he put his arm around her.

After a moment, Brian asked, "Are you?"

"Am I what?"

"Desperate? Just wanted to know for the record and all." His smile did not deter the slap he got on the shoulder.

"I am *not*. I'll have you know, *I* date the boy next door." The phone rang just as Brian leaned forward to plant a kiss on her cheek.

She answered it after a pause of hesitation.

On the line, she heard a voice she recognized. "I know Brian is with you."

Mrs. Henderson. Tessa refused to give her any fuel. "And, this makes you what? Good with a pair of binoculars?"

"You just have to find out on your own, don't you young lady?"

"You know what I *have* learned, Mrs. Henderson? I mean no disrespect, but your malicious gossip could really get someone hurt. Or get you in trouble."

"A snippy little thing, aren't you? That's Brian Miller talking. A smart mouth with no respect. I had thought you better than that."

"I really don't care what you think one way or the other; good night."

"Was that Mrs. H?"

She nodded. "She's still trying to warn me off you."

"She gets points for tenacity."

The call put a damper on the evening. The humor they shared elapsed into an uncomfortable silence. Both of them became so ill at ease she didn't try to get Brian to stay when he got up to leave.

Chapter Nine

"Alex! You're alive!" Tessa grabbed her older brother and, nice restaurant or not, smothered him in kisses right there in the lobby where no one missed the spectacle.

He pushed on her and held her at arm's length. "Did you think I'd died?"

"I wondered, yes."

The hostess approached. "For two?" She wore a knowing grin.

Alex cleared his throat. "Nonsmoking, please."

"My brother the doctor!" Tessa spoke in a loud voice to embarrass Alex.

It worked. "Can you please use your inside voice, baby sister?"

She hated being called a baby. "I could if I wanted to."

"I doubt it. I'm a doctor, do you know what that means?" He turned to the waitress who handed him a menu. "Thank you."

"Thanks." Tessa also took her menu in hand. "What does that mean?"

He pretended to study the large plastic-coated paper. "It means I know people who can put you away."

"Then you could take care of Joey. Please! Please put me away!"

He eyed her above the menu with an arched brow. "Not while I draw breath. How is the monster?"

"Oh, he's okay. He came in second again in the pet show."

"That's nice. Did you call Danni?"

"Oh, yes. She's thrilled."

They broke into good-humored conversation. Questions regarding jobs, friends, and family asked and answered.

"What's happening in your love life now that you're a full-fledged doctor?"

He put down his iced tea after a good long drink. "Nothing. There's no time. I love what I do, but I really wish I'd taken a different position. This one leaves me no time. No dates. No movies. I can't even enjoy a game without getting paged."

"I don't think I'd like that." She thought of Brian. He'd been paged a time or two since they'd been friends and more.

"You've got that look on your face, Tess. What's his name?"

No need to lie. "Brian Miller." She hoped she smiled properly and not with a wistful look.

Her smile, however, must not have done the trick.

"You don't look happy about it. What's going on?"

During their meal, Tessa poured her heart out. She explained all she recalled, right down to the Mrs. Henderson incidents. "I'm not sure what to do. He works out of town; where does that leave me?"

"Alone, at least some. I'm more concerned with this nosy woman across the street."

"I know. She gives me the creeps. I thought she was just a nice lady, but she's evil. She hates Brian with a passion. It all started with a baseball through the window when he was a kid."

"Then she'd have hated our block, huh?"

"Especially you."

His clear blue eyes flickered with concern. "There's more, isn't there?"

"I'm worried that this won't work with Brian."

He reached across the table and took her hand. "Tessa, is this guy worth taking a risk?"

"Oh, yeah, Alex. He's worth it. I'm crazy about him."

He took a deep breath. "This is so hard for me to say, but you've got to take a chance and trust him to do the right thing. You wouldn't love him if you didn't think he'd do what's right."

His words echoed in her head. She expected the best from Brian. She now had to learn a lesson of patience. "You're right, of course."

"I'm the oldest, I'm always right. Dessert?"

"I have to get back to school. I could only get out for lunch because we're having an in-service day."

He took the check and would hear no argument. "What good is it to be a doctor if I can't take my best girl to lunch?"

"I thought Danni was your best girl."

"Only when I'm taking *her* to lunch."

"My fickle brother, as always."

They got up to leave.

"Now that you're grown up, working you

against each other doesn't work like it once did."

"Remind me to shoot you at a later date. When I have more time."

"Sure." Playful sarcasm poured from his lips. "I'll leave the note with my assistant."

Brian did his best to concentrate on his meeting. There were extenuating circumstances, however. He'd just gotten back from lunch where he'd seen Tessa with another man. He was in this meeting changing his entire lifestyle and she was with someone else.

A tall, dark, good-looking guy who seemed to have her full attention. Especially when she kissed him.

At that moment, there was no focus, and he couldn't afford a missed step right now. Not one.

"Brian? Are you with me?"

"I'm sorry, Sherry."

"Jim's right. You are off your game."

"He told you that?"

She smiled kindly. "Oh, yes. But, he also said he thought the problem was a woman. I can see he's right about that part too."

Brian didn't breathe until she continued.

"The woman you brought to the Owens' party?"

"Yeah."

She sat back and tapped her pencil on the table. "Tell me about the woman you're willing to leave the road for. I've been waiting five years to meet her. She'd better be worth it."

"I've only known her a few weeks."

"But I knew sooner or later you'd want to settle down. And it's okay, but the least you can do is tell me her name."

He hesitated. Maybe Tess didn't want him. It didn't matter. He wanted her. "Tessa. Tessa Price. She teaches fourth grade."

"You love her, don't you?"

"Yes, I do."

Sherry cocked her head when she asked, "But you're not sure of her right now?"

He looked at the papers on the table before them. "I don't want to talk about that."

"Okay, but don't worry, Brian. It will all work, you'll see. Is Jim coming to this meeting?"

"Yeah. I haven't quite figured out why; this is my account. Do you know?"

"No, but I'll call him and tell him not to bother. He can't add anything to this discussion and there's no reason to overwhelm this company."

He checked his watch. "I need to call Tessa. I'm going to have to cancel dinner tonight."

He dialed his cell. He tried to sound detached, but once Brian had his ducks in a row, Jim had some explaining to do.

"Tessa? Hey, it's Brian. I won't be over tonight. I've got work."

"Oh. Okay, should I wait up?"

"Mm. Probably not."

Tessa heard a voice in the background. A woman's voice. "Are you ready, Brian?"

"Yeah. I have to go, Tess."

"Good night."

" 'Night, sweetie."

With the night alone, she caught up on some laundry and looked over lesson plans, comparing them to her goals for her kids.

When the phone rang a couple of hours later, she hoped Brian could still see her for a few minutes, though it was late.

"Is this Tessa Price?" She couldn't identify the male voice.

"Yes. May I help you?"

"I hate to be the bearer of bad news, but your friend Brian is out with someone else tonight."

Apprehension probably wouldn't have poured over Tessa so strongly, but she'd had a strange feeling when Brian called earlier.

"You think I care?"

"I know you do."

The call ending click resounded through her head. Unfortunately, she didn't have caller ID or other elaborate phone services that could trace the call.

She hated this situation. Nothing black and white, just a lot of shadows, and, in the end, no way to tell what was real.

Chapter Ten

After eleven o'clock Brian pulled into the drive. No lights on at Tessa's. No surprise. He'd been much longer tonight than he'd expected.

Much longer.

He had to admit he hated this evening. It hadn't been easy pointing fingers at Jim's work. Sherry had seen it now too. She'd put Jim on the spot and he didn't have a lot of answers for her.

But, Brian would get them.

"Brian?" The soft word came as a skiff on the spring breeze. Tessa waited on the porch.

He walked around to the front of her house. She sat in the glider, dressed in a light sweater and pair of jeans. "I feel guilty."

He kissed her forehead. "Why?"

"I'm afraid. I need to ask you something, but if I do, I'm afraid you'll answer me."

He sat down next to her, taking her hand in his. "Never be scared to ask me anything. Even if the truth's bad, we'll get through it together."

She sighed. "Were you at work?"

"Not exactly. But, I *was* working."

"Brian, we can't have secrets if we're going to be together."

"I have a confidence issue. I can *not* tell you anything at this point."

"Because you're seeing someone else."

"What?"

"I got a phone call tonight. A man told me you were seeing someone. He knew my name."

Brian had a pretty good idea where the call came from. "There's someone at this office who is afraid I'll get his job. I assume the call was him."

"And the woman?"

"I was with Sherry Beacher tonight. She owns the company. That's all, Tess. I can't talk about any of the rest of it. I'm sorry if the call spooked you."

"I'm a woman living alone and I get a prank

call from a man who knows my name. I admit, it's a little unsettling. Now that I know it's not an axe murderer, I think I'll go to bed."

He squeezed her hand in a good night gesture. Without a word, she got up and went inside.

Brian didn't leave Tessa's porch immediately. For a few moments he rethought all that had happened in the last few days.

He and Sherry had quite a talk after the client left the restaurant. She was almost as angry with Brian as she was with Jim.

She kept drilling him on what he knew. But, he had no hard proof of his suspicions, so he tried to downplay some of the issues that had reared their ugly heads this evening.

God, he was tired. He looked around the neighborhood for a moment trying to find some peace and—no. It couldn't be. Sure enough, Mrs. Henderson had her binoculars trained on him from across the street. He stared at her. Straight at her. So strongly was his glare that she started to waiver, then put the spyglasses down altogether.

Interesting.

He walked to his house and went inside. His father sat at the kitchen table eating ice cream. "It's in the freezer if you want it."

"No thanks. Your Mrs. Henderson gets under my skin, Dad."

"Now what?"

"She had a pair of binoculars watching Tess and me from her front window. No telling what will be around the block tomorrow. Then, there's Tess; she got a strange call this evening. Someone, probably Jim, tried to convince her I was with another woman."

His father appeared apathetic. "Don't worry, Son. She'll have to settle down soon."

Though in a foul mood, Brian chuckled. "Which one?"

Sam looked up from his bowl. "Both of them."

Like every other morning since she'd had the pets, Tessa put them on their respective leashes and chains and went back inside to get ready.

Her night left much to be desired. Today she would see what teaching with sleep deprivation would do to a person. With slow, articulate motions she went through her usual morning. Tessa took a shower, got dressed, did her hair in a ponytail, and put on some makeup to cover the bags beneath her eyes.

Back outside, she stopped short on the porch. Lilly smiled at her as she always did, but Joey wasn't on his chains. And, there had been two of them since his last escapade.

"Joey!" He didn't grunt, snort, or give her any type of answer.

Oh, no! If he got away, I'm dead. Danni's due home tonight.

She followed his hoof prints, but they led only to the drive and then stopped. Of course, no prints would be left on the tarmac. She followed the drive to the street and stopped. Panic rose in her throat, making her hoarse as she yelled his name.

Sam Miller came outside. "What's wrong, Tessa?"

To the point of tears, she asked, "Mr. Miller, Joey is gone; have you seen him?"

"He hasn't been in my flowers today." He patted her arm. "We'll find him, honey. We won't let anything happen to the little critter."

Feeling much like a child, she looked first down the street, then up the other way. "My sister comes home tonight. If he's gone, she'll never forgive me."

"I'll help you look, Tessa. Don't worry."

"I have to call a substitute teacher in to work for me. I'll be back."

She ran in, made her call, and, with leash in hand, met Mr. Miller out front.

Mr. Miller asked her, "Do you want to split up, or go together?"

"I'll look down this way." She pointed towards the place Joey had stopped to eat pansies that night. "If you don't mind going the other."

"Not at all." He smiled kindly at her and set out to do her bidding.

Tessa ran as fast as she could throughout the neighborhood, afraid at every turn she'd see Danni's beloved pet dead in the street.

Please, let me find him.

Over an hour later, she returned home to find Sam sitting on her steps.

He shook his head. "I've been from here to Eighth Street, but I didn't see him. I walked through all the yards on both sides of the street. I'm sorry, Tessa."

Though she wished Brian would join them, she knew he couldn't do anymore than they had. "I can't thank you enough for trying, Mr. Miller."

She ran back into the house and called all the local radio stations, asking them to announce over the air that the pig had run away. She was only able to obtain their help after explaining he'd placed second in the annual pet show.

Brian pulled into the drive. He looked as bad as she felt.

She walked out to meet him. "He's gone."

"What? Who?"

"Joey. He's gone. Your father and I searched the neighborhood; I called the police and the radio stations. Brian, my sister is due back tonight. If I don't find him, I'm afraid she'll never forgive me. To us, he's just a pet, but she loves that little piggy with her life."

Brian first rubbed his forehead, then his hand trailed back through his longish dark hair. "What else can we do?" He wasn't asking her, he was asking himself. He thought a long moment. "I don't have any other ideas, but if you want me to go back through the neighborhood with you, I will."

She nodded, but panic rose inside her.

Once again, Tessa—this time with Brian at her side—stalked through yards and over fences. They even knocked on doors. Most of the people that Mrs. Henderson was well acquainted with would barely speak to them, but no one admitted to knowing anything about Joey's disappearance.

They got back a couple of hours later, tired from the walking and the rejection. Tomorrow was the block party and most of the people who'd be there wanted nothing to do with them; that much was obvious.

But, above all else, Joey was still missing.

They sat on the steps of Tessa's home. Neither said a word, until she jumped up and yelled, "Animal shelter! Maybe someone had him picked up!"

She ran inside, made the call, and came back to where Brian sat. "No luck."

"He couldn't have just disappeared, Tessa." With determination he got up and walked to the chains that had held him. After a thorough examination, he spoke. "Someone unhooked him, Tessa."

"No. I don't think so. Remember the other day? He got free from the one chain—"

"Or did he?"

"Sure he did."

"I think you're wrong. I think someone kidnapped him. If someone knows who this pig is, then he could be worth a ransom."

"That's not logical. I don't have money. If I did, I'd live in West Port, not here." She referred to another part of town. The area in which Brian wanted to raise a family.

"You may not. But I'd say most of the people around here have it on good authority— Frieda Henderson—that your pig is from the

big court case a few years ago. There are probably people out there who think he's worth a
bundle."

"Danni and Mike would pay it too."

They were tired and worn out, but Tessa
stood. "I'm going inside. I'll make flyers on
the computer to hand out when I make my
next round."

"Call me, Tessa. I'll go with you."

"I will." Her sad smile made him want to
comfort her.

"Can I come with you?"

"No. I need to get them made so we can get
back out. You may want to change clothes
anyway."

He wore a suit from a breakfast meeting. "I
will. And, I'm staying home today to help
you."

She offered a sad smile. "Thanks." The
word came out as a croak and he knew she
choked back tears.

Without thought or words, he put his arms
around her, not caring if the whole neighborhood witnessed it. "It's going to be fine. We'll
find him."

Reluctantly, he let her go into her house.

He, too, walked inside. Before he got the
door closed his father was beside him.

"Tell me you found the little guy."

Brian shook his head. "We didn't. Tessa is heartbroken, and some of the people on this block were all but rude."

"And you?"

He sat down at the kitchen table. "I got things straight at work."

His father followed suit. "If this is how you look when you're right, I'd hate to see the loser."

"It was hard to expose Jim as an embezzler. After all, he hired me. At least I'll be working from this office in about three months. But at what expense? Jim and I had been friends until recently. I got him fired, Dad. He's lucky Sherry didn't press charges." He shook his head. "It was over a relatively small amount of money too. I can't believe he did it."

"But he tried to keep you out of this office."

"Of course he did. He knew my methods. He was afraid I'd find his bookkeeping tricks. I wouldn't have if he hadn't acted so strangely about the account."

"You built that business for them. He said it himself. You earned this, Son. Sherry sees it. Accept this and move on."

"I did all this for what? I know Jim had to be exposed, but do I even want to stay here?

Things may not work between Tessa and me. Why did I bother?"

"Why would you think things won't work out for you and Tessa?"

"I think there's competition."

"And, when you run up against competition, what do you normally do?"

Brian grudgingly smiled. "I win."

"See there?"

"What makes you so sure, Dad?"

"Because that gal has more than beauty and guts. She has brains. She'll come back to roost. I promise you that."

The phone rang. Brian got up and answered it.

"Brian, it's Tessa. If you don't mind, I need help passing out the flyers I've made."

"I'll be right out." He loosened the tie he wore from work and took it off. "I'm going upstairs to change. If Tessa comes in, just ask her to wait."

He changed into jeans quickly and met her outside on the front porch.

"I put a hundred dollar reward on there. I can't afford more, but if someone asks for more, then tell me. I'll come up with it somehow."

"I think you should stay here in case the phone rings. I'll do this."

She held Joey's leash and the flyers. "We can cover more ground if we split up."

"I'll get my dad to help me. You stay by the phone." As an afterthought he added, "What if your sister calls?"

She took a moment. "We could leave your father at my place."

"I really think *you* should stay. After all, you wouldn't want Dad alarming your sister on the phone."

Tessa looked a long moment at him. "You're right. Thanks, Brian. And, thank your dad for me."

He watched her turn and go back inside.

"I will, Tess."

He looked at the flyers, a picture of Joey and the reward amount along with her phone number. He went inside his father's and added a zero to the amount. The reward now stood at a thousand dollars.

With Sam's approval, they both set out to find Joey for Tessa.

While the men continued to search, Tessa stood near the phone, willing it to ring. When it did, Tessa jumped as if bitten, and answered it on the first ring.

"Hey, little sister! How are my babies?"

Danni.

"Fine." The lie burned like acid on Tessa's tongue.

Upsetting Danni wouldn't help matters at this point; Joey could be found any minute.

"Well, our flight was delayed; I'm sorry. We'll be home tomorrow afternoon sometime. Think you can keep things in order until then, Tess?"

"Sure, Danni."

A long pause followed Tessa's reply and she wondered if she'd lost her in the transatlantic call.

"Tessa, honey, are you alright? You sound different."

"Of course, Sis. It's probably just the fact we're thousands of miles apart."

"No, I hear you fine. It's that boy next door, isn't it?"

If you only knew. "Can we talk about this when you get home?"

Danni acquiesced. "For now, you're off the hook, but just wait until I get home."

Tessa didn't stop the small smile that threatened her lips. "Good. I'll talk to you in about twenty-four hours then."

"I love you, Tess."

"I love you back, Danni."

It wasn't uncommon for the women to talk to each other this way, but somehow, for Tessa, it meant more today. She knew if Danni came home and she hadn't found Joey, the relation-ship would get bumpy for a while.

The thought of things never being the same between them, possibly ever, made her nau-seous. *Please, let them find Joey for us.*

Chapter Eleven

When Brian and his father, after splitting up to cover more territory, met back at Tessa's porch, Brian could see the strain on his dad's face. He knew his own must echo the look. "No pig?"

Sam shook his head. "Son, that pig is smart and all, but he's not big enough to have gone far. Surely someone would call the police or animal shelter if they had a pig in their yard or garden."

Brian's voice held his frustration. "Tessa's going to be heartbroken."

Tessa came flying down the porch steps and into Brian's arms. "Did you find him?"

"I'm sorry, Tess."

Mr. Miller shrugged and walked away.

"Danni just called. I've got twenty-four hours before she gets home."

"She'll just have to understand."

"I know. Eventually, I'm sure she will. But she'll be so hurt. I just can't do that to her. I've got to find him."

Her cordless phone, strapped to her belt, rang. "Hello."

"Tessa, this is Mrs. Henderson."

"Hello, Mrs. Henderson—" Tessa stiffened.

"I saw your flyers. That's quite a reward."

Thinking the woman made fun of her hundred-dollar amount, Tessa retorted, "It's all I could afford."

"I think you're looking too far from home."

"What does that mean? Too far from home? Do you know where he is, Mrs. Henderson?"

"Why not ask your Brian? His father is the only one with reason to want to get rid of him." The phone clicked as Mrs. Henderson hung up.

Tessa did the same. She grabbed Brian's sleeve and pulled him into the house behind her, not saying a word until they were in the living room with all curtains pulled.

"Do you know where Joey is?"

"Me? Why would I travel all over the area looking for him if I knew where he was?"

"Mrs. Henderson said to ask you."

"Me? Did she say why?"

"She said I looked too far from home, that your dad is the only one with reason to want to get rid of him."

"Dad and I both know he leaves this weekend. With that in mind, why wouldn't we have done something to him sooner—when he really was a problem?"

Tears threatened. "She made fun of my reward."

"A thousand dollars is nothing to sneeze at."

Shock engulfed her. "A thousand? No, the reward is a hundred."

"I added a zero."

"I don't have a thousand dollars."

His tone curt, he glared at her. "No, but I do. And, if you still don't trust us, then feel free to come over to the house and look everywhere for him. Anywhere you want. Even in the drawer with my socks and boxers."

"I might just do that."

He stormed toward the back door. "Fine. I'll be there if you need me."

Alone with her thoughts, Tessa stayed near the phone.

If Brian and Mr. Miller know where he is, why go through with all the pretending?

Mrs. Henderson said they looked too far

from home. A certainty in the woman's voice gave Tessa the impression she knew where Joey was. The trick would be to get the old battle-axe to tell what she knew.

She took the cordless phone off her belt and dialed the woman's number.

"Hello."

"Mrs. Henderson, if you know where Joey is, then I'd advise you to tell me. He's not mine and this will upset my sister. Is that what you want? To hurt someone you don't even know."

"My dear, I've told you all I know. The only person in the neighborhood who has reason to want anything to happen to him is Sam Miller."

"Mr. Miller has helped me look. So has Brian."

"All an act for your benefit. I told you, they can't be trusted. They never could. Mr. Hall down the block said it—who else would want something to happen to him?"

Tessa's anger flourished. "You really are a bitter, lonely, old woman. Why would you do this? Where is Joey?"

"I told you. Mr. Miller has him, Dear. Now, I must go." She hung up on Tessa.

That witch!

Think, Tessa.

* * *

The block party is tomorrow. Brian sat on the window box in his sister's old room, looking at the stars. He'd left Tessa upset and near tears, but he wouldn't be called a thief. Not even for her. *Her sister will be home tomorrow. I don't know what she'll do.*

Mrs. Henderson. He looked towards her house. All lights off. Benign enough, but look closer and the binoculars occasionally hit the light.

If anyone in the area could be capable of hurting the little pig, it would be her. She didn't own a heart; just a piece of stone where it may have been years before he ever knew her. His dad tried to cut her some slack because her husband left her years ago and she'd always been alone.

A person doesn't have to be alone. But, a person does have to be a friend to have any.

He got up and walked downstairs, grabbing a flashlight from the utility room. Outside, he looked at Joey's chains. *That pig did not escape on his own. No. He had help.*

The back door of Tessa's house, bathed in darkness, opened. He heard the screen slam against the house.

"I'm sorry, Brian."

He reached forward and pushed a stray wisp of hair behind her ear. "I think I can cut you some slack."

She took his hand, holding it as she spoke. "Not one call. Not even for the reward."

"I suppose that means no ransom calls either."

"No. Nothing."

Releasing her hand, he knelt down onto his haunches to study the chains. "Did you file a police report?"

"Yes. I called the animal shelter before they closed too."

"One thing is for sure. Your little pork chop had help this time."

Her misery made its way into her voice. "We missed it before because we believed he'd done it on his own with his history." He stood up and dusted his hands on his jeans. "It didn't occur to us that he didn't."

"But, why then?"

Brian put his hand to the small of her back and gave her a wicked smile. "Because what does he do? He goes straight to Dad's."

"And I'm led to believe your father has him and that breaks us up."

"But, let's not forget the best part. This is all orchestrated by the wicked witch of the other side of the street."

"You two made up?" Mr. Miller joined the group.

Tessa looked at the ground. "I'm so sorry. I was stupid to believe anything that woman said."

Sam waved away her apology. "Don't worry about that, Tessa. When you called the shelter, did they say they could make sure he wouldn't get destroyed if he came in?"

"Actually, Fort White has a potbellied pig rescue that works with the shelter. If he gets taken there, they'll call the rescue instead of putting him down."

"Good." Sam appeared placated. "Is there anything else we can do?"

"I can't think of anything." Tessa said.

Sam turned to walk away. "I need my beauty rest. Good night."

" 'Night, Dad."

Brian turned his attention to Tessa. "You know how I feel about you, Tess."

"I know. The other night I just . . . I know things are crazy for you at work."

"I have had to make some decisions. One of them is to stay in Fort White." He squeezed her hand. "I want to be here, because of you."

"I can't talk about this right now. Not with Joey gone."

"Don't worry. I have an idea." He took her

elbow, guiding her towards the back door of her house. "Does your sister have any good friends, attorneys that would go out of their way for you?"

"I can think of one in particular."

"Excellent."

Chapter Twelve

Hugh Cramer answered the phone quite simply: "It's seven o'clock on a Saturday morning. This better be good."

"I'm so sorry, Hugh. It's Tessa Price. I need your help."

"Tessa?" She knew he remembered her. He'd known the family for years. "What's wrong? Is it Danni?"

"It's Joey."

He hesitated as if in thought. "The pig? Danni's pig?"

"Yes, Danni's pig. He's missing."

"You woke me up on my only day off in fourteen days for a pet? I'm a criminal attorney now, Tess. Unless he killed, robbed, or assaulted someone, I'm not your man."

"Hugh, be serious. Joey is Danni's pride and joy. And he's missing."

Grudgingly, he changed his tone. "I'm sorry. You're right. How's Danni taking it?"

"She's on her way home from Paris. I was pig sitting."

"So she doesn't know. Good for you. Because if you don't find the little hog, she'll never speak to you again."

"I need to get some advice from someone who won't tell Danni what happened. At least, not until I find him."

Hugh sighed. "Do you want to meet me at the office, or is the phone okay?"

In Hugh's office, Tessa and Brian explained their suspicions concerning Joey's disappearance. Hugh understood, as one of Michael and Danni's oldest friends, what effect this incident would have on the family.

He explained the possible criminal charges which could be brought against the person holding Joey. "Because of his background, Joey *could* be considered high cost property." Wearing jeans and a tee shirt, Hugh sat on the corner of his desk.

Tessa sat with Brian on a small couch in

Hugh's office. "But, if we threaten someone with larceny—"

Hugh's mouth twisted wryly. "It's not idle. If that's what you came here to find out, there's your answer. Joey is worth a ton of money. Especially since he's got those commercials under his belt."

"Any ideas on how we should handle this?" Tessa trusted Hugh's advice above anyone's right now.

He shrugged. "If it were me, I'd play good cop, bad cop."

Tessa sounded tired to her own ears. "Which means?"

Brian mischievously raised his brows as he looked at her. "In other words, one of us acts as if we're going to have her thrown in jail, and the other one pretends to take her side."

Her despair lessened as she realized she had some power in the situation. "I can do that."

On the way out to the car, Brian commended Hugh. "He didn't have to meet with us. He didn't have to help us, but he did. He must love you."

"Actually, he's crazy about Danni. He took her under his wing when she began her law career. He's still one of her closest friends."

"I half expected him to be the man I saw you with at lunch the other day."

Her mouth dropped open. "You saw me at lunch? With a man?"

"Yeah. No big deal, not as if it bothered me."

By this time they sat side by side in the front seats of Brian's SUV. She patted his arm. "You should have come to the table and met my brother Alex, instead of worrying about it."

He started the car. "Worry? You think it worried me? Nah, I just wondered who it was. I never worried about it."

"Good."

"Not one bit." He put the car in drive. "Just one of those things a person doesn't think twice about."

"So I see." She offered him a kiss on the cheek.

"I can pull over, if need be."

"Drive, Brian, just drive."

When Brian and Tessa pulled beside the house, the block party was in full swing, with everyone on the street out to play. Even people Tessa hadn't met had barbeques and tables set up on their lawns. Children raced in the streets, running, skateboarding, in-line skating—all there to enjoy since the street had been roped off, except for residents, for traffic.

She hoped someone had left a message on her phone, but there weren't any when she got inside.

"Should we go to confront the adversary now, or take a break first?"

Tessa thought it all out in her mind. What would happen, what could happen, and what had already happened. "I have an idea. You may not like it, but I think it will work for several reasons. I need your dad to help."

"That won't be a problem. I think he's almost as upset as you are."

This will work.

Brian and Sam set out their grill, like all the others. Tessa joined them at their table with cookies, fudge, brownies, and other snacks.

Neighbors walked between the homes and greeted each other. A few people came by their table; they didn't seem to know Mrs. Henderson well. There were still a few homes she hadn't penetrated.

Brian called next door to his neighbor. "Mrs. Weathers! It's so good to see you."

She barely spoke. "Did you find the pig yet?"

"No. We have an idea what's happened but only the police will be able to tell us for sure."

Sam chimed in. "How's Barb?"

"My daughter? She's fine. Thank you for asking."

Sam continued innocently enough. "The baby fine too?"

"How did you—?" The woman looked towards Mrs. Henderson's house. "All is well, Mr. Miller."

"Sam. You can call me Sam."

Warming up to him, she offered, "Would you like some fudge, Sam?"

"I'd love some. Frieda told me your fudge was only second to her own."

Mrs. Weathers huffed. "I doubt that. I've won several blue ribbons in the county fair, and she's never even placed."

Tessa saw Sam had this one under control, so she went the other way. On the other side of her house were the Harrisons. She'd play her way into their hearts.

"Hello!" She called to them as she approached them.

She received a cool greeting. "Did you find the pig?"

"No. Not yet." She placed a couple of brownies on their table.

"Mrs. Harrison, could I speak with you a moment?"

She pulled the woman aside. "Mrs. Henderson told me all about you and your husband's problems. If I can help in any way—"

The other woman gasped in surprise. "Our problems?"

"According to her, you two are ready to break up."

"Not at all! We had a spat one day when she stopped by, that's all."

A sigh escaped Tessa's lips. "She can really blow things out of proportion, that one."

The other woman's doubt apparent in her voice, she added, "Like you and Brian in your driveway?"

"Do you know she keeps binoculars to check out the neighborhood when she thinks no one's watching?"

Mrs. Harrison peered at the house across the street as if looking for proof. "Are you serious? How do you know?"

"I've seen them."

The woman's countenance relaxed. "Please call me Joan, and feel free to take one of my angels. I make them every year for this. Different colors to mark the occasion."

"Thanks, Joan. That's so sweet." She took the offered gift and studied it. What cute angels they were, made from yarn, sparkles, and beads. "This must be the blue year. I have just the place for it."

"You're welcome. I'm sorry if we've

seemed . . . standoffish. That woman." Joan referred to Mrs. Henderson.

Curiosity got its best of Tessa. "What exactly did she tell you?"

The blush that entered the woman's cheeks told her it wasn't good. "I can't even say it; just that you two had no shame."

"We did kiss." Tessa admitted it so Joan would know the truth.

"I suppose when she decided no one would care in this day and age what you'd done, she spiced it up. A lot."

With finality in her voice, she explained her position to Joan. "I'm not letting her back in my home. She's done so much damage to Brian and myself. And now Joey is gone. She called me to tell me Sam had him."

Joan laughed aloud. "Sam Miller is a nice guy and wouldn't hurt your pig, Tessa. I know he can be grumpy, but like my husband says, at that age, we'll all be that way."

"I didn't think he did it. I just wish I could find who did."

"I thought he ran away." As she spoke, Tessa saw the wheels of her neighbor's mind turning.

"No, I had him on two chains. He definitely had help."

"I'd say there's only one person on the block who talked about him." Her gaze didn't waiver from Tessa's.

"Mrs. Henderson."

"One and the same. I don't know how mean she really is. Only how she talks. I think you'd better get him back soon."

Tessa held up the angel. "Thanks, Joan. I'm glad things are good with you."

"Let me know if you need any help."

Chapter Thirteen

By the time Tessa, Brian, and Sam drank lemonade on Tessa's porch, people didn't meet with Mrs. Henderson at the table on her lawn. They'd spent the entire morning crushing all of Mrs. Henderson's stories with the truth and revealing her lies regarding others on the block.

This time, Mrs. Henderson stood alone.

"It's getting late." Tessa broke the silence as she looked at her watch. "Almost four o'clock."

Sam took a sip of his drink. "The people with the big field in back of their house, what's their name?"

Brian filled in the blank. "Raines."

165

"That's right. They're having fireworks as soon as it gets dark. We should be able to see them from here."

Again, silence overtook the small group. They waited. They watched. They knew eventually the plan would come to fruition.

When it did, of course, they wouldn't need a field for the fireworks.

Mrs. Henderson strode to her next-door neighbor. After a few moments, they heard shouting. Not able to hear the words, but the body language spoke for itself.

The gossipmonger was not welcome there.

"Do you think she'll know who told them the truth?" Tessa asked.

Mrs. Henderson turned and stormed toward them.

"It appears so." Sam put his drink on the wicker table. "You kids have fun. I've got work to do."

He got up and shuffled into Tessa's house.

In what appeared to be an effort to catch her breath, Mrs. Henderson paused before she stomped onto the porch. "Who do you two think you are? And, you!" She pointed to Brian. "Where is your father?"

Brian stretched and yawned. "Dad has some business he needed to attend. Is there something I can help you with?"

"You are a lousy, good for nothing cheat, Brian Miller! That's all you'll ever be!"

Tessa remained calm. "Have a seat, Mrs. Henderson. I'll get you some lemonade if you like."

"Lemonade? Are you out of your mind, young lady? Don't you see the damage you've done?"

"Damage?" Brian asked the question. "Damage? Oh, you mean we told someone you were in a fistfight and evicted from your apartment. You mean that type of damage? Where one person is put on the line and ruined all because someone else doesn't like that person."

Tessa took note of her surroundings. Their adversary may not realize it, but the whole neighborhood had stopped in mid-motion to hear and see what would happen.

She hoped the show wasn't too extravagant.

Mrs. Henderson made an apparent effort to stay calm. "You were evicted from your apartment—"

"My apartment was vandalized. You didn't ask. You just thought of the worst case scenario and told it as truth."

Tessa, grateful she didn't shake when she picked up her glass, gave Brian a sidelong glance. "What about Brian's job? You never knew what he did, so you made it up."

"You were always a cheating, lying little kid, and that's all you'll ever be!" In a rage, Mrs. Henderson picked up the lemonade pitcher and threw it on the concrete stairs. The liquid and glass scattered all over the steps and walk. She turned to leave and froze.

The entire neighborhood watched.

She slowly took each step and made her way back to her house, her head held high. Not a soul spoke to her. The woman didn't look from side to side, but stared straight ahead at the door of her house. Once there, she shut it behind her.

Possibly, Tessa thought, for a long time.

A moment passed before anyone moved. One by one, conversations began and the party once again became jovial.

"I'll get that later." Tessa saw the lemons and glass smattered in front of her. "I want to check on Lilly."

Brian followed her inside.

The dog lay on the couch, all four paws straight up in the air.

"He's not back yet." Tessa sat down next to Lilly and rubbed her belly.

Brian took the chair opposite her. "He'll be back in a few minutes."

"What if he's not?"

"He will be."

Silence availed. Tension hung in the air.

Finally, the door opened and Sam entered the house by himself.

No pig.

Tessa jumped up from her seat. "She didn't have him?"

"He's in the basement. I could hear him, but couldn't find a way in."

Suddenly, Lilly perked up, jumped from the couch and ran for the door. She jumped, scratched, and all in all tried to get outside.

Tessa didn't understand why until the door opened.

Danni.

"Tessa!" Danni rushed to her sister and threw her arms around her. "Oh, it's so good to be home. I've missed you so much!"

As cold dread coursed through her veins, Tessa hugged back and echoed her sister's words. "You look great! I'm so glad you're home! Have you seen Mom yet?"

"We came straight here. I'm worn to a frazzle. Thought we'd catch the families tomorrow. We're still operating on Paris time."

Tessa, at a loss for words, looked at her sister's tired features. In a few moments, she'd be so hurt.

Tears threatened.

Brian offered his hand to Michael. "Brian Miller. I live next door." He pointed to his father. "My dad, Sam."

Tessa motioned for everyone to sit down. "I didn't expect you back until later this evening."

Michael provided the reason. "The airlines are so shaky. You never know when your flight will be delayed or pushed up. So, here we are." He stroked Lilly's back as he talked.

Danni spoke to Lilly as if she were a person. "Is your brother outside in the yard?"

Brian interrupted. "I've been to France a few times, where did you stay?" He'd steered the conversation away from Joey. Thank God.

Michael talked about the beauty and difference in culture before turning to Tessa. "You know, Sis, it's been so long since I've just had a drink of good water. Do you mind if I get one?"

"Allow me." Tessa got up and strode into the kitchen.

When she entered the room, a soft knock on the backdoor surprised her.

"Hi." The man from across the street, next to Mrs. Henderson, was on her back porch. "Tell Sam the old battleaxe left and we can get into the basement if we need to. My eight-year-old son can get through the window."

"I'll have him meet you. Thanks. My sister is in the living room right now—"

He nodded understanding. "Sam told me the story. We'll be waiting."

Tessa prepared a pitcher of iced water and glasses on a tray and took them into the living room. "Sam, I almost forgot; Mr. Raines said he had a way to get that item you've been looking for."

He raised a brow. "Then I'd better go get it."

Brian stood as well. "I'll help you."

After the men left, Danni and Michael showed off picture after picture of France.

Michael chuckled. "Believe it or not, we still have film we haven't developed."

"Not to mention," Danni added, "the camcorder video."

"It looks as if you've had a wonderful time. Do you plan to go home or do you just want to bunk here tonight? I'll make you breakfast, even if it's at noon."

"No," Danni's appreciation evident in her reply, "we just want to get our critters and go home."

"Where's Joey?" Michael asked.

Tessa spoke too quickly. Certainly they'd know the truth just listening to her ramble. "Outside on a chain. Let me tell you about your son, Joseph Sommers. He has been treated like the little prince you've made him out to be. Long walks, grooming, bathing, and all the things you'd expect in a piggy resort. I've had to chase him a lot though." She turned directly to Danni. "You know how he is when I have him. He runs every chance he gets. Sam Miller, he lives next door and has the most beautiful garden. I don't think anyone enjoys it as much as Joey does."

Danni's hand flew to her mouth. "Oh my! He was here though; he couldn't be too angry about it."

"He's been nice. Really. The first few times he said nothing. Then, he kind of eyed me funny. Then he sent Brian over to talk to me about him."

Danni leaned forward—her mind off the pet and on Tessa's love life. "Is that how you met the hunk?"

"I resent that, counselor." Michael stated flatly.

Tessa sat back while the two of them went into one of their mock trials. It was a game they enjoyed, and, to be honest, Tessa almost always learned something about the law when they did this.

You two just keep talking. Play your little games and talk for hours. Just give them time to get Joey back before you know he's gone.

When Michael excused himself to the restroom, Danni became more inquisitive.

"This Brian guy is a real cutie, Sis. What's the story?"

"I think we're going to make things work, Danni."

Danni scrunched her nose. "Funny. You don't seem too excited about it."

"There are always hurdles to jump. You know that better than anybody."

"Oh, yeah. Speaking of jumping, let's bring Joey in so I can adore him while we chat. I'm sure he's missed that."

"I don't know. I *try* to adore him and I took him to school where the children *did* adore him. Plus, there was the pet show where he won another ribbon."

Danni got up from the couch and strode to the back door. "It's not the same thing as his mother."

Tessa tried to stop Danni as best she could by getting between her and the door. "Speaking of children, in your condition should you even be outside where dogs and pigs, among other things, roam?"

"Tessa! You're acting strange. Is something wrong? Is Joey alright?"

"Of course. He's fine. It's not like he's really a kid, Danni, he's just a pig. Right?"

"Step aside, Sis. I want to see my pig."

Michael entered the room. "What's the problem?"

"Mike, I think Tessa is hiding something. She won't let me outside to see Joey."

The back door opened. Brian stepped in. "We're having some neighborhood fireworks. Why doesn't everyone come out to see them?" His smile, precious to Tessa, meant good news.

The group followed him and there, chained to the tree, was the precocious porker. Danni and Michael bathed him in scratches, strokes, and belly rubs.

All was well.

Too tired for much else, Danni and Michael took their "family" and went home. Tessa didn't try to get them to stay.

Good fortune decided to smile on Tessa because Danni and Mike had gone with their pets before Mrs. Henderson came home from wherever it was she'd flown on her broomstick.

Chairs lined Tessa's side of the street, as it would be the best place to see the fireworks. Neighbors were excited and mingling. Some wearing heavy sweaters and others wrapping up in afghans, as the blackberry winter had temperatures in the low forties.

Mrs. Henderson slowly pulled into her drive and garage, closing the door behind her. Tessa and Brian eyed each other, knowing in a few moments the fireworks really would begin, and it would have nothing to do with colors in the skies.

Brian took her hand and whispered, "Don't be mistaken; this will be the best day of your life."

"Does that include the confrontation we're about to have?"

"Don't let her ruin this day for you, sweetie. You'll see. It's going to be a wonderful evening."

"How can you possibly say that knowing the obvious?"

"Because I planned it that way."

Mr. Raines owned a fireworks store. He sat back next to Sam's chair, and, with a walkie-talkie in hand, told the people who actually handled the boomers what he wanted. "We'll get started in about five minutes, everyone! Get your seat or anything else you might want to eat or drink now; this is your warning!" He yelled out so everyone could hear him, his voice cheerful.

Tessa heard him tell Sam, "Even though I've been planning this for a couple of months, I've never wanted to do things for the people here before. Now that we all know what that Henderson woman has been doing, it feels good to stand together and help each other."

Gladness flooded her. She'd said some things today that made her feel wrong, guilty, even as she'd dispelled some of the old woman's gossip.

"My house has been burglarized!" Mrs. Henderson stood on her porch screaming. "Someone broke into my home!" She stomped down the steps towards Brian and Tessa. "You! You did this! You broke into my house."

Mr. Raines spoke into his radio, "Hold on for a few minutes, guys."

Brian beamed at her. "How do you know someone broke in, Mrs. Henderson? Is it vandalized?"

"You know that's not how I know."

"How *do* you know?" Tessa asked the question, then took a sip of hot chocolate. "Is something missing?"

"Missing?" Mrs. Henderson stammered, "N-No, nothing of importance."

Sam Miller stood up. "I was in your home. I took back the pig you stole from Tessa."

All those assembled gasped collectively.

The murmurings from the fifty or so people were clear in Tessa's ears. "She stole her pig . . . the one she looked for all day . . . how could someone do that?"

"It's not true!" Mrs. Henderson yelled. "I didn't have the pig."

"Yes you did." Mr. Raines looked up at her from his seat. "I helped Sam get him from your basement. Tessa's sister had already returned home. But, you could have caused some real damage in her family by stealing the little guy. You didn't care, though, did you?"

Tessa could have heard a pin drop when Brian took over. "Tessa, remember you can press charges if you want to, and your sister is an attorney. She could take her to the cleaners on civil charges alone."

Mrs. Henderson ranted and raved, making little sense. Mostly about Brian. Then, about Tessa and Brian.

"Just stop!" Tessa stood; the afghan she had on her lap fell to the ground. She looked squarely at the woman. Tessa allowed her anger to flare. "You've lied. You've even stolen. On top of that you made me out to be some kind of . . ." She paused. "Maybe in your eyes, I am. But, to be perfectly honest with you, your opinion means nothing to me. I see you as a lonely old woman with a malicious heart. You're not welcome in my home." Tessa sat down and fixed her blanket back on her lap.

Brian put his arm around her. "Oh, and please call the police. I'd love nothing more than to see Tessa press charges for grand theft."

The woman turned on her heel and marched back to her house, slamming the door behind her.

"You played the bad cop really well." Tessa poked Brian on the shoulder as she spoke, trying to relieve some of the tension in the air.

"I wasn't playing. I think you should consider it after all she put you through."

"No. It needs to end somewhere. Here is as good a place as any."

Mr. Raines, who refused Brian's reward money, got the fireworks started. It eased the strain in the audience as the sounds and colors flashed through the air.

Brian and Tessa snuggled happily in their chairs beneath the blanket.

"Okay, boys," Mr. Raines spoke into the radio, "do the special one."

Brian held her tighter as red hearts danced in the sky and the words MARRY ME TESSA played there with them.

Tessa, though surprised and delighted, only snuggled closer. "The answer is yes."

"Good, then I won't have to carry this

around anymore." He slipped a beautiful solitaire diamond onto her finger.

"I love you." A tear trickled down her cheek.

"Now the world knows you belong with me. Of course, I've known it since your pig got in the flowers."

"That is the most romantic thing any man has ever said to me."

Brian kissed her on the forehead. "I've got plenty more where that came from."

They noticed then the fireworks had stopped and no one else moved or spoke. All eyes were focused on them.

Brian looked around. "She said yes."

They all applauded the occasion and the show resumed.

"I told you this would be the best day of your life. Remember, I'm never wrong."

"Never wrong? Well, we'll see about that one."

Epilogue

The evening sun made for a beautiful lighting that couldn't be matched by any artificial means. Almost all their neighbors had come to see them joined together along with their families.

Brian wanted to run down the aisle to meet her, but held himself at bay. This day would make them one, and though he asked for patience, it eluded him. Seeing her like this in the white gown, train, and veil shook him to his very core.

Their eyes never left each other, their gazes locked together as the minister read their vows and they repeated them back for him and the congregation in the park to hear.

"Have you the rings?" the reverend asked.

Joey marched proudly up the aisle, his blue collar shown with a crystal case that held the golden circles.

Brian removed the case and the ceremony continued.

People commented at the reception what a unique idea it was to bring the animal into the ceremony.

Tessa answered some unspoken questions. "Some may think it wrong, but that's why we chose the park instead of a church setting. Joey is responsible for us meeting and falling in love. We couldn't keep him out."

Joan Harrison, dressed to the nines, came up behind Tessa. Brian heard her whisper, "Mrs. Henderson is here."

He watched his bride go to the woman, her smile genuine. "Mrs. Henderson. I'm glad you came."

"I will admit, Tessa, it surprised me to get the invitation."

"I hope you enjoy yourself."

Uncertainty laced the woman's voice. "I'm sure I will. I noticed the little pig had your rings. That was certainly . . . different."

"Yes, it was."

"I'm moving. There's a place for old women like me out on Kingston Pike. Even though you tried to make things better for me, most of the neighbors . . . well, let's just say I'm not welcome anymore. I hope you can forgive me. I don't know what else to say."

"Then get some punch and cake and say nothing. Just enjoy the people around you without judgment." Music started to play. "I have to go have my first dance with my new husband."

"Tessa?"

Tessa turned back to look at her. "Yes?"

She offered a small smile. "Congratulations."

"Thank you. I hope you have a grand time this evening."

"I wish you and Brian all the best."

Tessa nodded as she turned back to Brian and glided into his arms. They took the area set up as a dance floor and danced to an old Elvis Presley love song.

Brian pulled Tessa close to him. "Paul tried to talk me into the university's fight song for our first dance."

"But you wanted to live long enough to get to Cancun for the honeymoon."

"You were very kind to that woman after all she did. You could have had her put in jail. All you did was tell her off."

In her smile he saw beauty, life, and his future. "Forgiveness cleanses the soul."

"And love?"

"Love keeps the soul living."

"Then our souls will live forever, Mrs. Miller."

"Forever." She agreed with a kiss.